3:16

By

Jeffrey Martin

Cold Moon Press
USA

ISBN: 978-0-578-07039-1

10 9 8 7 6 5 4 3 2 1 First Edition

First Printing October 2010
Printed in the United States of America

3:16

By

Jeffrey Martin

Dedication

Sometimes a man can meet his destiny on the road he traveled to avoid it. These words have great meaning to me as I embark on the next installment to this writing journey. I spent my young adult life blinded about what God had in store for me and have come to realize each of us has a gift to share with this world...and I thank him for the ability to create stories which pique the interests of readers.

So without further ado, I thank Lisa, my wife and safe haven from the trials and tribulations we encounter on a daily basis. Thanks to Katie, Kelley (my #1 Southern fan), Rick, Jen, Kenny, Connie, Lorry, Nurse K, Lisa, and all of my Facebook and MySpace fellow authors and friends. I appreciate your devotion to my vision.

Brandon Thornley unzipped his jacket and removed the GPS device. Following the frost-covered trail, he reached the wooded sanctuary that was home to the tools of his *real* trade. He thought he could give it up and live the life of an honest man, but the hunger for killing was *too* strong and couldn't be masked any longer. He forced himself through the dense tree branches, barely feeling their backlash on his exposed face and neck. A few steps further, he stopped in front of a large pine tree. The computer-generated voice from the GPS, which indicated he had reached his destination, startled him.

Wonderful...nobody had found my hiding place. Brandon dropped down to one knee and used both his hands to dig away the earth hiding his prized possessions. *Ah, there you are.* Reaching into the exposed hole, he pulled out a medium-sized brown leather pouch. His pulse quickened as he fumbled with the clasp. *Easy...you've got this.* Taking a few deep breaths, he slowly opened the pouch, reached inside, and pulled out several cloth-wrapped items. He unrolled the first, and the most beautiful double-edged blade he had ever set eyes on glistened in his grasp. Brandon repeatedly ran his fingers along the knife's length, worshipping the texture and the craftsmanship of the weapon. All the other knives in the pouch were equally exquisite, and *all* were very capable of carrying out what he needed done, but Brandon had a special place in his heart for this one. *Sort of like a good friend coming back into my life*, he thought.

He looked down at his watch and knew he would be pressed for time. Carina would be planning a late evening dinner, and she would expect him soon. Placing everything back into the pouch, he carefully refilled the manmade hole.

Brandon scurried back to the late model Mercedes, unlocking it. His cell phone was on the travel charger, and he snatched it up, preparing to call his wife. The red notification light blinked. *Hmm, looks like a message.* His finger flicked across the touch screen, and he realized it wasn't a message, but it *was* something interesting.

Brandon had recently joined a social networking site in hopes of reconnecting with old friends. The site had the option to add the application to his cell phone, which he had done almost instantly. The red light indicated someone wanted to add him to his or her friends' list. He opened the request and noticed the person wanting to be a part of his networking world was someone named Cassie Youngblood. There was a profile picture of the young redhead, and Brandon thought he noticed something else. He moved his finger in a downward motion and smiled when he wasn't mistaken in what he had seen. Cassie Youngblood was a local girl who lived very close to Brandon; unfortunately for her, it would be too close.

Perfect timing, he thought. Brandon pulled the Mercedes onto the street, considering all the potential victims the social networking arena could bring…

CHAPTER ONE

Brandon grasped the stainless steel blade, prepared to carry out his deadly agenda. The red-haired Cassie Youngblood was only a few yards from him. Brandon was astonished how beautiful she was in person, compared to her profile on the *Konnect2u* web site. Her figure was accentuated by the tight, dark blue sweater and the off white capris. She was sitting at a picnic table with several textbooks spread out in front of her and appeared to be using that as a front for the *real* focus of her attention. It appeared to be a copy of *EyeSpot*, the latest tabloid magazine.

Brandon lifted his pant leg and tucked the knife back into its sheath. He smoothed his graying hair and straightened the charcoal suit. Satisfied with his appearance, he stepped out from behind the long row of eccentric sculptures.

"Hello, Ms. Youngblood." Brandon could tell he startled her.

"Oh, hello, Mr. Thornley. I was just studying." Cassie smiled as she slid the magazine inside her backpack. "Thank you for coming. I really enjoyed your blog about corporate security and violence in the workplace."

"Ms. Youngblood, now you're just lying to me." Brandon laughed.

"No, I'm really serious about this career path. That's why I e-mailed you to meet me today. It would be cool to learn some pointers from you."

Brandon took a seat across from the girl and glanced at the books on the table. "Well, if that's the case, I have something special in mind...if you are interested."

Cassie Youngblood wasn't a naïve woman, but a quick peek at the man's ring finger made her feel a little more at ease.

"A special exclusive from the head of security for the largest threat assessment company in the Midwest...maybe the world? Of course I'm interested." Cassie haphazardly piled the books into her backpack.

"Okay, you don't mind taking my car, do you? It's a little walk, though. I don't have a parking pass, and I had to leave it a few blocks away."

"No, I don't...mind riding with you," Cassie said nervously.

"Great. Maybe next time, I'll let *you* drive." Brandon smiled, trying to ease her doubts on his attentions.

He led her down to the secluded parking lot where only a few cars remained. *Make sure nobody is paying attention*, Brandon thought. He led her to the passenger side door, opening it.

"There you go."

"Thanks, Mr. Thornley." Cassie noticed the plastic draped throughout the car's interior. "A little cautious with your car, *are you?*"

"Not really. Children, you know...they aren't the neatest of individuals." Brandon took her bag and placed it on the backseat. "Another thing. Call me Brandon. I think we can be on a first-name basis. After all, you did contact me on *Konnect2u*, right?"

Cassie flashed him a playful grin. "Yes, I thought it was pretty cool that you were on there."

"Well, I admit, I was honored to get your request, but I have to tell you something."

Cassie turned towards him, a half-serious look on her face. "You have my undivided attention, Mr. Brandon Thornley, Security Guru."

He stared down at his watch. *It was close to the deadline...time to end this charade*. Brandon reached into his jacket, and before Cassie Youngblood realized what he was holding, a portable stun gun sent fifty-thousand volts shooting through her, sending the redhead into a state of unconsciousness. When he was satisfied she was still, he made sure she was propped upright in the seat. Brandon even buckled her safety belt, trying to make sure everything appeared normal, though he doubted anyone would pay attention to his passenger as he traveled through town.

Brandon pulled the car into traffic, almost getting sideswiped by a truck full of Christmas trees. *Well, that's the wrong way to avoid attention.* He drove for several minutes until he arrived at the destination reserved for this special ritual.

Reaching over his motionless guest, he flipped open the glove compartment. He removed a CD from its holder and slid it into the car stereo. Soon, the interior was filled with the sound of rolling waves that searched for a home on some unknown shore. Brandon briefly closed his eyes, savoring that peaceful visual. When he opened them, he was drawn to the blue digital clock display on the disc player. It was *time* to satisfy the hunger within.

Brandon lifted his pant leg and unsheathed the polished knife. He scooted closer to the young woman, running his fingers over her freckled face. Leaning in, he pressed his chapped lips against her cheek.

"Don't worry. I'll make sure to take good care of you."

Brandon raised the blade, repeatedly invading Cassie Youngblood's flesh, until the plastic seat covering was streaming with crimson, and his appetite—for the time being—was satisfied.

CHAPTER TWO

Brandon double-clicked the laptop's mouse, and within a few seconds, the request to add a new friend to his list had been sent. *Cindy Palentine, you are the next contestant on Thornley's Game of Death.*

His youngest son burst through the office door, interrupting Brandon's thoughts. "Dad, come on...you said, you was gonna play a video game with me a hour ago—"

"Ryan, I'm almost done here. Just give me a sec, kiddo," Brandon said, his eyes scrolling down the web page.

"Mom says I gotta go to bed soon. She says I need to be extra good cuz Santa's coming in a few weeks."

"She's right. I almost forgot." Brandon flashed him a devious grin.

Ryan hung his head, slowly walking towards his father. "What's you doing anyways?"

Brandon quickly minimized the screen, turning to meet his son's curiosity. "Work stuff...nothing fun. I'll be done in a few minutes, and we can finish the game from yesterday."

Ryan eyes lit up. "Really? You're not kidding?" Ryan then put on the most serious look a nine-year-old could manage. "Okay, Dad...just two more minutes?"

Brandon smiled, trying to hide his displeasure that his son had barged in on him during his *special* time. "Yes, two more minutes, and we can play."

"Pinkie swear, Dad...you gotta pinkie swear." Ryan held out his small hand.

Brandon laughed as the two interlocked fingers. "You satisfied now?"

Ryan flashed a smile. "I'm gonna beat you so bad, you won't want to play me *ever* again."

"We'll see about that." Brandon stood up from the chair and walked the well-fed boy to the door. "Just two minutes Ryan…that's all."

Ryan stared at his wrist, pretending to look at a watch that wasn't there. "I'm *counting*, starting *now*…one, two, three…"

Brandon shooed him out of the room, trying hard not to smile at the boy's persistence. Then, he locked the door and rushed back to the laptop. He typed in a few words, and a list of potential friends popped onto the screen. Brandon scrolled down the page until one particular picture captured his attention. The background for the design was red with a heart directly in the center. It was black, and a large two-headed snake surrounded the Valentine's Day symbol. Below, was a name new to the web site. Brandon gazed at it for a few minutes before deciding to check it out further. *Donovan Petrie, you just might be a suitable friend.*

Ryan returned to the office and was banging on the door. "Dad, it's been two minutes. Come out!"

Brandon looked once more at the member profile for Donovan Petrie before he clicked on the button to request him for his unique list. He logged off and shut down the system, then got up and opened the door. His impatient son was holding a wireless game controller.

"*See*, I told you it would only be a couple of minutes," Brandon said, escorting his son away from the office and away from his secret world.

* * *

Donovan Petrie sharpened his knife as he stared at the young, naked woman across the table. Jamie Brooks was the blonde-haired vixen and inept waitress from the neighborhood restaurant. She was known for abusing her good looks to get whatever she wanted. Those looks, however, had been altered by Donovan's steel blade. Her blonde hair was now mixed with streaks of blood, as each cut in her scalp produced a river of the precious liquid. The blood had started to pool beneath her chair, seeping into the cracks of the broken tiles. Donovan reached out and snapped his fingers, waking her from her trauma-induced state.

Donovan yanked on the circular metal attached to her skin, and the force caused it to bleed. He smiled at the piece of surgical steel. "Hey, wake up, bitch."

Jamie Brooks blinked her eyes, but it was more of a reflex than anything else.

Donovan slapped her across the face. "Hey, you can't die...not *just yet.*" He looked at the girl and removed the gag from her mouth. "I bet your ass *you* figured you'd be in some poor schmuck's bedroom *instead* of here tonight." Donovan laughed, hitting her again in the face. This time, he used the knife, and blood sprayed in all directions.

"Please don't...no more." Jamie forced out all the words she could.

Donovan cocked his head, adjusting his glasses. "So, you want to beg now? I remember when I was begging you for a date...and you laughed like I was a piece of shit. I don't think so. Begging doesn't suit you...not at all."

The blonde woman tried to use her waning strength to escape the chair, not realizing the chains were holding her in place.

"*Some* people like restraints. Sort of *another* reason I use them." He laughed, pulling on the chains. "I guess you don't, huh?" Donovan stepped behind her, forcing them to dig further into her flesh. "Hey, *you're* no fun. Maybe I should just slice you up, and be done with it."

Jamie opened her eyes and stared at her captor. The pale, skinny man was coming at her again, and she could do nothing. Donovan positioned the blade against her throat. He leaned in and took a sniff of her hair. The mixture of spilled blood and melon shampoo was making him overly excited. He pressed the blade tighter against her supple skin, preparing to end her life. He inadvertently glanced down and noticed a red, blinking light on his phone.

"Jamie, don't go anywhere, I have to see who this is," Donovan joked, placing the knife on the table in front of his victim.

He retreated from the woman, flipping open the phone. *Hmm, looks like someone wants to be my friend,* he thought. Donovan enjoyed the local *Konnect2u* networking web site, and any request he received to be someone's friend, he was sure to approve. He smiled, recognizing the name of the person who wanted to be added. Donovan hit the yellow approval button and closed the phone. *Thank you, Mr. Brandon Thornley, thank you so much.* Donovan turned to Jamie Brooks as he grabbed the knife from the table.

"Okay, *you're* really no fun at all. But guess what? I think I found someone who might enjoy my company." Donovan walked behind the girl and took one final smell of her hair, setting the blade against her jugular. He whispered in her ear. "You don't have anything to say before we are done here, do you?"

Jamie Brooks whimpered, but no intelligible words came out.

Donovan shrugged his shoulders. "I guess not." He jerked the blade from left to right, watching the arterial spray from Jamie Brook's body erupt all over the small kitchen. He stood up, flipping the knife on the table. *I hope my new friend is more of a challenge than this one...*

CHAPTER THREE

Homicide Detective Patrick Morgan flashed his shield at the young officer stationed at the yellow barrier. The run-down apartment complex on North Haven's south side was known for domestic disturbances and the occasional drug bust, but *never* in his fifteen years of policing the community had Patrick been called for anything like *this*. He glanced down at the silver name badge of the officer.

"Officer Herde, any word on who our victim is?"

"No, Detective. Commander Cromartie is waiting for evidence techs to take her fingerprints."

"Okay, do we have anything on witnesses as of yet?"

"Just one, sir...the elderly man who discovered the body."

"Where is he now?"

"He's in apartment 213. Officer Gren is taking his statement."

"Good. Is Commander Cromartie on scene?" Patrick asked.

"Yes, he's been here for about twenty minutes. He wanted me to let him know when you arrived."

My daughter's appointment was my first priority, Patrick thought. "Thanks. You better radio him and let him know I'm here...wouldn't want to get *both* of us in trouble."

"Will do." Officer Herde's smile faded. "How's Kelsey anyway?"

"She's hanging in there. Doc keeps telling us she's almost old enough to repair the hole in her heart, but Herde, she seems to *always* be exhausted."

"Keep the faith, sir."

Patrick shook his head. "Herde, *I* don't believe in faith, but thanks anyway." He paused. "Hey, one more thing. When the evidence techs arrive, send 'em up." Waving to the officer, he entered the dimly lit hallway.

The area was empty, except for two malnourished cats sharing the remains of a headless rat. *This place needs to be condemned*, Patrick thought. He walked down the hallway until he reached apartment 106. The door was wide open, and another New Haven police officer blocked the entrance. Patrick made eye contact with him, and the sadness in the man's eyes spoke volumes.

"Sir, the apartment belongs to a Wheeler Hodges. Commander Cromartie has an *All Points Bulletin* out for him. Doesn't look like he's been here in a while."

"Probably not, but you never know." Patrick patted him on the shoulder. He barely was inside the apartment when the combination of spilled blood and stale vomit made his nostrils flare.

"Detective Morgan, glad you could join us tonight." Commander Cromartie's towering figure came out from another adjoining room. The former defensive lineman from Iowa State stared down at Patrick.

"Yes, sir. I wouldn't want to miss the chance to get in on *this*," Patrick lied, knowing the Commander could sense bullshit sincerity a mile away.

"Come over here. I hope you got your big boy panties on. This is one fucked-up crime scene. Dumb ass even left the murder weapon on the table—"

"What?" Patrick looked puzzled.

"Yes, you heard right…not too bright a guy that did *this*." Cromartie threw a small bundle at him. "Put these on, and follow me. Be careful…damn lights are burnt out."

Patrick slipped into the white plastic shoe covers. The investigators stopped in front of a partially broken kitchen door.

"You ready for this?" Cromartie removed the mini-light from his belt.

Patrick nodded.

"Here we go, then." The senior investigator pushed open the door, aiming the flashlight towards the center of the room.

Patrick saw the outline of the square table, and the knife Cromartie had mentioned was close to falling off the edge. *"Holy shit,"* he whispered.

The new source of light was a welcomed comfort since the only other illumination came from four dark candles placed on the floor surrounding the victim. *Showcasing his prey*, Patrick thought. The naked body of a once-beautiful woman was sitting chained to a wooden chair. Patrick inched closer, trying to step over the pools of blood. He stopped a few feet away from the young woman, almost overpowered by the stench of the dead.

Leaning down, he shook his head in disbelief. *No fucking way*. This crime was heinous enough, but with the addition of his next discovery, the bar was raised for what was *truly* sinister. There were matching circular wounds on the top of each foot with streaks of red marking the path of each puncture on her skin. Patrick could barely see the steel tip of the nail heads. *She never had a chance*.

"Did you see this shit?"

Cromartie wiped a hand over his wrinkled brow. "Bastard used a nail gun. That's just plain fucking evil."

Patrick reached into his jacket, pulling out a plastic evidence bag. "Hey, take a look at this."

"What is that?" Cromartie raised his eyebrows.

"Looks like a piece of meat, maybe the remains of our killer's dinner." Patrick made sure he had the latex gloves on before he scooped it up and slid it inside the plastic. The CSI geeks would be more than a little pissed if he ruined their chances of collecting the killer's DNA.

"Geesh, are you kidding? He stopped to have a goddamn lunch break before he killed her—"

"Unless he fed it to her, for some reason," Patrick said, staring at the chains imprisoning the woman.

"Yeah, right. I'm betting Hodges hasn't cleaned *this* shit hole since he moved in." Cromartie pointed in the direction of the bag. "*That* has probably been there for months."

"Maybe." Something caught his eye, and he bent closer. "Whoa, boss, look at these chains." Patrick motioned for Commander Cromartie to join him. "Take a look right *there*. Some other metal appears to be intertwined with the chain...do you see that?"

Cromartie leaned in. "What in the hell is it?"

"From the looks of it, I would say it's barbwire."

"Barbwire?"

"Yes, it looks like something the killer put together himself." Patrick pointed to several lacerations on the victim's wrists. He stared at the fingernails of the dead girl. *Manicured and very well taken care of*, he thought.

Cromartie ripped off his tie and stuffed it inside his front suit pocket. "A fucking creative killer who did well in shop class with nail guns and barbwire? What the hell..."

"Commander, this place is a mess. Odds are when he slashed her throat that blood got on him as well." Patrick reached over with a gloved hand and inspected the knife. "Okay...why leave this at the scene?"

"Because, Morgan...the freak is insane and could give a rat's ass about getting caught."

"Then, sir, there should be some nice juicy fingerprints just waiting to be discovered on this," Patrick said, lowering the evidence into a brown paper bag.

"Morgan, I'll get the night shift patrol officers checking the local bars, and we might as well check the twenty-four-hour superstores. Mr. Hodges, if he *is* responsible, may be recognized by the clerks."

Patrick shrugged. "By the looks of the place, boss, Hodges isn't coming back."

"You're probably right, but he's still the only lead we have."

"Something else. The dead girl isn't from around this part of town, either. She has a recent manicure, and the polish looks to be the expensive type."

"Prostitute?" Cromartie cocked his head.

Not surprised he would say that, Patrick thought. "No. Besides being in this place, she doesn't fit the kind of girl someone around *here* could afford."

"Morgan, she's from *somewhere*."

"And when we found out where, maybe *that* will tell us how she ended up *here*."

CHAPTER FOUR

Brandon Thornley pushed his way through the glass double doors of Langston Security Solutions. It was recently rated one of the largest threat assessment trouble shooters in the Midwest and was becoming the dominant force in the security industry. The majority of people living in New Haven believed it was only a matter of time before the organization outgrew the mid-sized city and decided to relocate.

It was this background working as a federal law enforcement investigator that made him Langston's best choice for their open position of security director. That was over ten years ago, and since then, he had made *quite* a name for himself. The countless magazine articles, radio interviews, and online blogs had propelled him to the top of the industry.

Brandon made his way to the oversized security desk. The red and green garland was strung from one side to the other. Former New Haven Police Officers Monty York and Trisha Gregory alternated between checking identification badges and providing visitors with much-needed information. Monty was a twenty-year veteran of the department, and his stocky build made Brandon think of his instructor at the law enforcement academy. Trisha Gregory was a petite woman in her late twenties and a recent victim of sexual harassment from her former department. Brandon honestly liked the two.

"What's the good word, troops? I see we decorated." Brandon smiled.

"Sir, did you see the newspaper this morning?" Trisha ignored his comment on the holiday décor.

"No, I was busy with the office in Sacramento. What did I miss?"

Trisha's small frame stepped out from behind the desk. "Mr. Thornley, there was a murder last night. It's been the morning buzz around here."

The city always has murders, Brandon thought. "Ah, morning gossip for all."

Monty York reached behind the desk and retrieved a folded copy of the *New Haven Minute*. He snapped it open, pointing to the headline. "Right there, boss."

Brandon skimmed the news story with interest. *That's why I bury the bodies.* "That's not too far away," he said.

"About eight minutes south. We used to have drug calls all the time." Monty shook his head. "First murder there in a while, though."

Monty will have some information for me. Brandon glanced over at Trisha. "I want to talk to Monty upstairs...it won't be long."

Trisha knew when she was being left out but was well aware her supervisor did have a stronger bond with Monty.

"Okay, sir."

Brandon flashed a smile. "Not long, I *promise*."

The two men turned down the hall and entered a private elevator. A few minutes later, they were sitting in Brandon's office on the fiftieth floor.

"Monty, so there's *more* to this murder than the paper is reporting?"

Monty leaned forward in his chair. "You know there always is, but you're not gonna believe this."

If you only knew, Brandon thought. "Well, share with the class...please."

Monty gripped the sides of the chair. "My friend who runs the Crime Scene Identification Unit was even freaked out."

"That bad?"

"He said the crime scene looked like some sort of ritual. Candles all around the dead girl." Monty cringed. "That's not *all*...her feet were nailed to the floor."

Interesting technique, Brandon thought. "It does sound gruesome."

Monty grew red in the face, shot up from his chair. "The bastard didn't stop there, sir. He slashed the poor girl's throat…like she was some filthy pig going to slaughter."

Brandon appreciated the man's emotion. *I could never feel like that.* "Anything else your friend told you?"

"Yes, apparently the killer left the murder weapon at the scene—"

"What?" *This guy really wanted to get caught*, Brandon thought.

"Damn straight. He left it there. I just don't get that." Monty tapped at his head.

"Well, tell your friend if their investigators need the video from our exterior cameras, I would be happy to help."

Monty nodded. "I'm sure he'll appreciate it. He won't be too happy I told *you,* though."

"I can keep a secret if you can." Brandon put a finger to his lips.

"I didn't do well with the one I just told *you.*" Monty forced a smile.

"True, but sooner or later, everything you just said will show up in the media anyway…don't you think?" Brandon cocked his head.

"Yes, sir. You have a point there."

Brandon peeked at his watch. *Time to get rid of my guest.* "Monty, I have a meeting in a few minutes. Head back down to your partner and give her a hand." Brandon waved as Monty exited the office.

When he was alone, Brandon eased the desk open and pulled out the black piece of headwear. It was worn, but he didn't care. The mask was part of him, and he *needed* it.

Brandon laid it on the table as he booted up his desktop and logged in. *Great to have such resources.* With just a few clicks of the mouse, a list of his favorite web sites appeared. He double-clicked one in particular, and his home page was replaced with a green screen requesting his password. After his access was approved, Brandon typed in the name of person he was looking for. Thirty seconds later, a picture of a middle-aged woman, along with her current address, was staring back at him.

Brandon ran his fingers along the outline of the woman's picture, and a chill went through his body. *Hello, Cindy. I can't wait to finally meet you...*

CHAPTER FIVE

Detective Patrick Morgan took a sip of the hot chocolate, scrutinizing the statement of Thomas Quinn. The senior citizen was the first person to discover the girl's body, and so far, his written account of the event was less than helpful. Patrick tossed the useless paper into his inbox. *Maybe later this mumbo-jumbo will make more sense.* He stepped out from his cubicle in time to see Commander Cromartie heading his way.

Oh, great...what does he want?

Cromartie handed him a folded piece of yellow paper. "Morgan, just got a call from Missing Persons. They received a report of a girl fitting our victim. Get over there, and get a statement."

"You coming?"

"I have to meet with the Chief. Give me a call if it's anything," Cromartie said.

Patrick flipped open the paper. *Hmm, very expensive neighborhood.* "I told you she didn't belong in that part of town." Patrick smiled.

"Yeah, yeah, do you want me to bow to your fucking brilliance?" Cromartie turned and walked off.

* * *

Patrick parked the unmarked car on the adjacent street in front of 5830 Alpine Avenue. A second unmarked Ford pulled up behind. The driver approached him.

"Detective Morgan, I'm Detective Steve Wilson...from Missing Persons."

He exited the car, extending his hand. "Call me Patrick. Can you give me a little intel before we go in there?"

"Sure, we got a call from a Serena Owens. She reported her live-in girlfriend, Jamie Brooks, hasn't been home in two days. Serena says she left here wearing a white trench coat with a red sweater and blue jeans."

"The girl was found nude. CSI team didn't find any clothes in the apartment." Patrick rubbed his day-old beard.

"Serena also said Jamie's parents have been leaving messages on the machine, wondering why she hasn't returned calls." Steve Wilson shrugged. "A coincidence?"

"Maybe it's not? Let's see if we can get anymore from her."

Patrick followed the other investigator to the front steps. Patrick knocked, and the dark-haired athletic figure of Serena Owens was soon in the doorway.

"Ms. Owens, I'm Detective Morgan, and this is Detective Wilson. We need to ask you a few questions about your roommate."

Serena's eyes appeared bloodshot. "Yes, please come in. Sorry I look like a mess."

Patrick smiled. "No problem. I'm sure it's been a difficult time."

"Yes. She hasn't called, and I can't sleep knowing she may be hurt." Serena led the detectives through a massive hallway and into an untidy, windowless dining area. Motioning for them to take a seat, she took an active role to clean the area.

Patrick decided it was best to let her keep herself busy while they conducted the interview. *The girl is on the edge of a breakdown.*

"Serena, this won't take long…just a few questions to follow up on what you told the officer over the phone." Patrick flipped over to a clean page on his legal pad. "Has Jamie lived here long?"

"We moved in over three months ago. I bought the place for us," Serena said, straightening the newspapers on the table.

Rich girl buys her lover a house, Patrick thought. "Did she have any ex-boyfriends or girlfriends who might be jealous of your relationship?"

"We *both* dated several men and women before we finally got together."

Patrick jotted down a few lines. "Okay, anything out of the ordinary happen lately? Maybe an ex-boyfriend *or* girlfriend contacting *either* of you out of the blue, for no particular reason?"

Serena, finished with her cleaning façade, finally sat down. "Well, I can only remember one thing, but it didn't seem like anything…"

"Go ahead; tell me what you can." Patrick touched her arm.

"Last Friday, I came home from running errands and noticed a strange tan car in our driveway—"

"You remember what kind?" Patrick's pen was poised.

"It was older…reminded me of the ones the state troopers used to drive."

Chevy Caprice, Patrick thought. "Okay, anything else?"

Serena wrung her hands. "Yes, the driver said he was lost and just pulled in to turn around. I got a bad feeling from him… *you* know what I mean?"

Yes, I do. A person's first instinct should be taken seriously, and Patrick wanted to dig deeper. "Can you remember what he looked like?" Patrick glanced at Steve Wilson.

"I'm sorry…things are just a little fuzzy." Serena shook her head.

"I know…but try if you can."

Serena sighed and clutched at her hair. "One thing that stuck out was the color of his skin."

Wilson leaned in. "You mean his race?"

She shook her head. "No, I mean the *color* of his face…it was like really pale. Looked like he was sick or something."

Patrick scrawled a few notes on the pad. "Let's stop for now, Serena. Just one more thing before we take off, okay?"

"Yes, Detective?"

"We want to take a quick look at Jamie's and your room. Is that okay?" Patrick smiled. "There might be something there to help us understand why she's gone."

"If it'll help find her, I'll do anything you ask." Serena wiped at a tear. She almost stumbled as she led the two investigators up the ivory staircase. Serena opened a set of cherry wood doors.

Patrick stared at the interior with envy. The two women had spared no expense on their pleasure, and the life-sized sculptures of mythical goddesses were example of this. The romantic setting *did* possess an oddity or two. All the walls were black and white checkered and covered with framed prints of another mythical being.

The girls must like pink, Patrick thought. He made quick eye contact with the other investigator, as Serena smiled at the curious gesture.

"Yes, Jamie *loves* pink unicorns so much, she went out and got a tattoo of this one." She pointed to one of the pictures.

"Excuse me, Serena...a tattoo?" Patrick stared at the cartoon-like design.

She turned around and tapped the back of her neck. "Yes, right here. It's just a small one, though. Pretty hard to see if you're not looking for it."

Shit! Patrick had inspected the victim, and there weren't any signs of tattoos or any other body art on her. "Serena, is that her only tattoo?"

Serena blushed. "Yes, but there is something else...both of Jamie's nipples...are pierced."

Jamie Brooks wasn't the girl at the apartment, Patrick thought.

"Serena, can you step out a minute? I want to talk to Detective Wilson."

"Sure, I have to call her mom again anyway. If you need me, I'll be downstairs."

Patrick closed the door, in case Serena was still in earshot. "Steve, the girl doesn't have the piercings *or* the tattoo. This isn't *her*."

"Shit. Maybe the killer ripped out the piercings?" Steve grimaced.

"I was *there*. Lots of blood, but nothing like that. Let's talk about the tattoo on her neck." Patrick reviewed his notes from the murder.

"They have that laser removal shit now...anybody can have one taken off." Steve shrugged.

You gotta be kidding me, Patrick thought. "No, the CSI team would have caught it—"

"So *you* still have a Jane Doe, and *I* still have a missing person's case?" Steve rubbed his eyes.

"It appears that way, but something else is bothering me."

"The guy in the tan car?"

"Yep. I wonder how many houses around here would have video surveillance."

Steve smiled. "Probably all of them."

"Good place for you to start. May help find this girl." Patrick opened the door.

Steve followed him. "What are *you* going to do?"

"Going to check with the medical examiner." Patrick felt the vibration from his cell phone, then answered it. "Yes, sir?"

The deep voice of Commander Cromartie filled the speaker. "Morgan, I need you to meet me at 2121 Barnt Street. I just found out who our Jane Doe is—"

"Who?"

"She was the daughter of *Magistrate* Regan Stephans. Apparently, she had been receiving threatening phone calls from a former boyfriend."

"Sounds like a prime suspect to me," Patrick said.

"Yes, or so you would think...problem is, he's dead as well."

"Are you fucking kidding?"

"I wish that was the case. He was found *nailed* to his shower wall last week."

"Nailed?"

"You heard right? I'll tell you more when you get here." Cromartie ended the call, leaving Patrick with an ocean of unanswered questions.

CHAPTER SIX

Detective Patrick Morgan assumed New Haven's most prestigious magistrate would live in the best neighborhood money could buy but was surprised when he pulled in front of the modest one-story. The chipped paint and unkempt yard made it a definite eyesore compared to the surrounding multi-million dollar palaces. Patrick spotted Commander Cromartie pacing around his unmarked vehicle. Cromartie looked up, hustling towards him.

"About two hours ago, we got a call from Magistrate Stephans. She indicated our Jane Doe is her daughter, Roxanne Stephans. There hadn't been any contact with her for a week." Cromartie handed him a sheet paper. "*These* are a list of threatening calls to the residence, prior to her disappearance."

"From the ex-boyfriend you mentioned?" Patrick asked.

Cromartie shook his head, pulling out a notebook from his shirt pocket. "Yes, the kids name was Justus Alleandro. It sounds like a history of domestic abuse with the two of them."

Justus getting justice, Patrick thought. "Not *anymore*. How did you find out about *his* death?"

"His parents found him in his Davenport apartment. They called here and told the magistrate about the murder." Cromartie loosened his tie. "Then she called us."

"*Davenport*? A goddamn long way from New Haven. Same method of operation for the deaths. *Someone* hated those two," Patrick said.

"Shit, Morgan, they were young kids. No fucking way did they deserve this…*no* fucking way."

"Is Magistrate Stephans still in there?" Patrick pointed in the direction of the house.

"No, she just left for the Medical Examiner's office. I told her to contact us when she's up to it."

"Hopefully, if there is any evidence, it won't walk away by then," Patrick snapped.

"Morgan, I called Davenport Homicide and asked them to send a copy of the report on Justus Alleandro. Maybe, there something in it, which could help us—"

"Before, anymore people are killed," Patrick handed Cromartie his notebook. "Check out the last page."

Cromartie flipped to the last page, scanning the contents. He crossed his arms over his chest. "Another missing girl? Do you think she just took off or something *else*?"

Patrick scratched his head. "Serena Owens was freaked out by a guy driving a tan Caprice."

"A lot of people buy retired patrol units. I wouldn't take much stock in this."

"Maybe, but she had almost a scared look in her eyes when she told us."

Cromartie rolled his eyes. "Her girlfriend hasn't come home; of course *anyone* strange in the neighborhood will get her fears going." He tossed back the notebook.

"Boss, I think we need to look at this before we just write it off."

Cromartie sighed. "Agreed. But first, let's try to take care of what we have right *here*."

"Gotcha, I'm gonna check around the house and see if there is anymore evidence on this Alleandro subject."

"Knock yourself out. If you *do* find something, hit me up on the cell."

Patrick glanced at his watch. "I doubt Wheeler Hodges has anything to do with this."

"Probably not. Just keep me posted, and I'll meet you back here at 0700 tomorrow," Cromartie called after him.

Patrick flipped to the back page of the notebook and re-read the description of the man Serena Owens had provided. Something about *him* had given her an uneasy feeling. Patrick knew Commander Cromartie could think whatever *he* wanted, but Patrick was a strong believer of trusting his instincts, and *they* were telling him the evil in New Haven was just beginning.

CHAPTER SEVEN

Donovan Petrie sat at the table, admiring the store's newest book seller. Tamara Bowers was a petite, thirty-something blonde with ivory skin and an electric smile. The trademark black polo and tan pants almost fit her like a second skin. Donovan watched while she climbed up a wobbly ladder, having difficulty balancing an armload of books. Donovan smiled at her independence. The woman possessed good enough looks to have any of the pimple-faced high school workers help her, but it appeared she wanted to prove this particular task was something she would do on her own.

Donovan took a sip from his mug, savoring the taste of the fine whiskey he had snuck past the mall rent-a-cop. *Yes, liquid courage is my weakness,* he thought.

Tamara took a glance in his direction, noticing he was staring at her. She flashed him a smile as she continued to put the inventory away. Donovan knew he wasn't considered good-looking or even average, so *any* woman who gave him the slightest attention was a boost to what little ego he had. He lowered his head, pretending to be interested in the headlines of the local newspaper, then realized his latest body of work was the hot topic of the day. *Wonderful, I'm getting some press.* Donovan folded the paper and shoved it inside his jacket.

He finished his drink and was about to get up when a hardcover book landed next to his foot.

A soft voice called down to him. "Excuse me, but could you hand me that?" Tamara Bowers started to descend towards him, but she lost her balance and slipped.

Donovan intervened and caught her before she hit the ground. He held her for a moment, then righted her so both feet were on the floor.

"Um, thanks…I'd have broken my neck." Tamara's face was flushed from embarrassment. She managed a grin as she straightened out her clothes.

"We can't have that." Donovan scooped up the misplaced book and handed it to her.

She brushed the hair out of her eyes. "Well, thank you…twice."

"No problem." Donovan started to walk away.

"Hey! What's your hurry?" Tamara followed him.

"I have to go."

"Can I at least reward you for a good deed?" Tamara twirled her hair.

The blood seeping from your body will be reward enough, he thought. "There's no need for that, but Mrs. Bookseller, be careful next time—"

"You can call me Tamara." She bit her lower lip.

I already know your name, he thought. "I'm Donovan. Maybe next time you can buy me a coffee or something."

She touched his shoulder. "Consider it done. Thank you again."

Donovan took a quick look back at the woman as she watched him leave the bookstore. Pushing through the glass doors that led directly out of the store, he walked around the side of the mall where the bookstore had reserved parking spots. He had had been doing his research on her and knew her preferred choice for parking. *There it is.* Donovan kneeled down next to the passenger's side rear wheel and removed a carving blade from inside his jacket. He looked in both directions, thankful for the cover of twilight. When he was satisfied there wasn't anyone in the area, he forced the rusted steel deep into the rubber. The hissing sound of escaping air put a devious smile on his face.

Donovan put the knife back inside his jacket and scurried back to his vehicle. *Nothing else to do now but wait.*

He opened the arm rest and grabbed his cell phone, logging into *Konnect2u*. Donovan skipped through the invitations for frivolous games and quizzes but decided to do a little background research on *his* newest friend. He scrolled over Brandon Thornley's profile picture and clicked. On the *information about you* section, he made mental notes as he read it from top to bottom. *Very high profile guy.* Donovan knew it would be difficult getting to him, considering the man's background, but a challenging kill was *just* the thing he needed.

Donovan had spent so much time learning about Brandon, he almost didn't realize what time it was. He looked out the window and noticed the lights from the bookstore's sign had gone dark.

"Shit." He threw the phone in the glove box.

Donovan turned on the engine and drove to the rear of the building, keeping his distance. He noticed the Durango was still parked in the same spot, but the owner wasn't anywhere in sight. *Fucking great…I missed her.*

As he was about to leave, he noticed the thin frame of Tamara Bowers walking across the parking lot. Stopping at her SUV, she noticed Donovan's handiwork. She slammed her purse against the pavement, then leaned up against the vehicle.

Looks like she needs my help again. Donovan laughed. He pulled away from his hiding spot and headed towards her. When he was about twenty feet from her, he stopped the car and flashed his lights.

Tamara shielded her eyes. She picked up her purse and quickly dug though it until she found what she was looking for. Donovan drew the vehicle closer but stopped when he saw her actually hurry towards him.

"Hey, asshole, turn off the brights," Tamara yelled, aiming the can of mace in his direction.

Donovan rolled down the window and smiled. "Asshole? Ouch, that really hurt."

"Oh, sorry. I didn't know it was you." Tamara covered her mouth. She lowered the can.

"How many assholes are you expecting?" Donovan stepped from the car.

"No, I don't...mean you. What are you doing here, anyway?"

"Had some mall shopping to do." Donovan changed the subject. "Looks like you could use some help."

Tamara half smiled. "Yeah, someone fucked up my tire. You have great timing."

"I didn't know book nerds had *that* many enemies." Donovan laughed, looking at the wheel.

"Hey, be nice," she scolded.

Donovan bent down. "You got a spare?"

Tamara shook her head. "Damn ex-husband took it."

Hmm. Nobody to worry about at home. Donovan glanced at his wrist. "It's too late to get it fixed. You need a lift somewhere?"

Tamara blushed. "It's the second time you have rescued me."

Donovan opened the passenger side door. "So, you owe me *two* cups of coffee."

"You'll have to come back and see me to collect." Tamara touched his arm.

"It's a date then."

Donovan pulled the car into traffic. Several minutes later, he was on the expensive south side of the city. Once in her community, she pointed to a beige house on the opposite side of the street where he'd turned.

"Do you want to come inside for a drink?"

Donovan stopped the car in front of the house. "No, I have to be at work early tomorrow." *After I kill you*, he thought.

Tamara stuck her tongue out. "I'll see you again soon, *right*?"

Sooner than you think. A smile crossed his lips. "Of course. I'll be in for that coffee you owe me."

Tamara bit her lip. "Well, thanks again...for *everything,*" she said, stepping away from the car.

"See you at the bookstore," Donovan said, leaving her standing on the edge of the curb.

A few blocks down was a twenty-four-hour eatery. He surveyed the area before parking at the rear of the building. Donovan popped the trunk and rummaged through the contents, slipping on a black nylon backpack. *Here we go.* Reaching into his jacket, he removed a silver cigar case and flipped it open, smiling. *I'll have one now and save the other for after.* Donovan zipped up his jacket and walked in the direction of Tamara Bower's house. *Ready or not, here I come…*

CHAPTER EIGHT

Brandon Thornley had decided to take a day from his busy schedule to attend to his next victim. Cindy Palentine worked for Blaisedale Reality, and her resume for finding houses for New Haven's wealthy was *most* impressive. She had just finished her fourth showing of the day and was driving her red Jaguar with reckless abandon, trying to get to the next.

Can't blame the woman for wanting to succeed. Brandon picked up his cell phone, tapping the numbers with his finger.

"Blaisedale Reality, Cindy speaking."

The soft but strong voice had almost an intoxicating effect on him. "Hello, Mrs. Palentine, this is Brandon Thornley. I sent you an e-mail on *Konnect2u*…about the open house on Shall Street."

"Great to get your call, Mr. Thornley. I'm standing in the kitchen of the home right now. It's simply lovely."

Such a liar. Brandon laughed. "Well, I hope so. My wife treats her kitchen like a sanctuary…and it's *almost* as big."

"Indeed. I can tell you first hand that the marble floors and oak cabinets make a perfect combination," Cindy said.

Hmm, always trying to close a sale, Brandon thought. "It does sound pretty amazing. I'm just running a few minutes behind but should be there soon."

"Excellent. I'll be waiting."

"Thanks, I can't wait to see it." He clicked the phone off.

Brandon took a glimpse down at his watch. *It'll be dark soon, but there's still time.* He turned the corner and headed in the opposite direction of where the open house was scheduled. After driving for several minutes, he finally stopped on a side street across from his destination.

Brandon scanned the neighborhood for several minutes until he felt confident his presence had gone unnoticed. Behind the passenger seat was a medium-sized brown paper bag. He grabbed it and stuffed it inside his coat, exiting the car. There were no vehicles in the driveway, and the walk around the house was quick and uneventful. At the back door, he fumbled in his front pocket, pulling out a thin piece of metal. Brandon inserted it through the lock, wiggling it back and forth until he heard a click.

Too easy, he thought, reaching down to his belt, unclipping the tactical flashlight. Brandon gently pushed the door open, aiming the light through the darkened interior. There was an intermittent beeping coming from the room adjacent. *Probably have sixty seconds.*

Brandon quickly located the alarm panel. *Bad choice of systems*. The L.E.D. on the white rectangular pad was flashing. *Gotta work fast*. He ripped out the paper bag from inside his jacket, removing several items. He inspected the screws, holding the panel in place. These were standard make and model, not specially designed for this particular system. The person who installed it was obvious naïve in the field. He peeked at the timer on the display.

Thirty seconds left. Brandon picked up one of the tools and removed each screw with skill and precision. The silver base plate loosened, exposing two black wires. He reached for the next tool, stripped the wires, then crossed one set of copper over the other and tied them together, wrapping them in place. The noise from the panel ceased, creating an eerie silence.

With the face cover secured back in place, he punched in a series of numbers, clearing the screen. Satisfied the system was ready, he reset the timer, then rushed through the house and out the door from which he came. Brandon checked the handle, ensuring the locking system was undamaged. *Excellent*.

Within a few minutes, he was sitting back in the driver's seat of his car. He reached out for the cell phone and hit the redial button.

"Blaisedale Reality, Cindy here." The voice sounded annoyed.

"This is Brandon Thornley. I had a car problem, but I'm coming now."

"Mr. Thornley, I'm going to have reschedule. Sorry, I have another appointment…want me to pencil you down for later tonight?"

That won't be necessary. "Mrs. Palentine, I'll check my schedule and get back with you. I didn't mean to cause you a problem."

Cindy sighed. "Well, I hope the house is still available tomorrow."

She's playing with me. "I hope so, too. That kitchen sounds perfect for my wife."

"Give me a call when your schedule is free. I'll *try* to keep other potential buyers at bay until then. I think once you see the house, it will be love at first sight," Cindy soothed.

She talks a good game. "Can't wait, Mrs. Palentine."

A devious smile filled his face, as he sat and waited for darkness. In a few short hours, Cindy Palentine would be buried in a shallow grave next to all his other victims. *Konnect2u* was proving to be a most precious ally in the quest to rekindle a hobby, lost…but not forgotten.

* * *

Cindy Palentine turned the Jaguar up the street, tired from a long day at work, followed by an after-hours party at a local nightclub. As she approached her house, a look of contempt spread across her face. *Mark forgot to turn on the timer for the damn lights.* She yanked the remote control from the visor, hitting the button. The metal scraped as the garage door slowly opened, exposing a steady glow. *At least this light works.* Cindy was about to exit the car, when the familiar sound of "Rock City" came screaming from her phone.

"Shit!" She fumbled for her phone. "Hey honey, guess what you forgot to do?"

Mark Palentine's voice sounded strained. "I hope nothing."

"*You* forgot the timer for the lights. You know I hate coming home to a dark house—"

"Huh? I checked the timer before I left—"

"Mark, I don't want to hear it. The damn lights are off, so that means you didn't check it."

"Cindy, I'm sure I did—"

"*Whatever.* I'm too tired to argue with you. I just want to take a nice hot bath and fall into bed." Cindy sighed.

"Late *night*? Or should I say early morning?"

"Fuck off, Mark."

"Maybe *I* did forget. I just called to tell you...won't be home, until the day after tomorrow—"

"You told me *tomorrow*...why do you have to stay?" Cindy exited, slamming the car door behind her.

"I have a meeting with the vice president of marketing tomorrow night."

Asshole. She pushed the button on the wall as the garage door started to close. "We have cruise tickets."

"I know, but what do you want me to do? He *is* the vice president."

"Mark, I told you about this. It's important we spend time together...especially since, it's damn close to Christmas. Don't *you* care?" Cindy stopped at the back door, placing the key into the lock.

"I care, but this is my job—"

"That's what I always hear. I gotta go." She threw the door open. It bounced hard against the wall, causing a picture to crash onto the floor. "Fuck!" She flicked a switch as the overhead lights flickered on. *Finally, some light.*

"Cindy, wait—"

She flipped the phone on the table. "Serves you right. Now I have to clean up this mess," Cindy mumbled to herself. She scrambled to locate a broom and dustpan. A few minutes later, she was emptying the remaining shards of glass into the trash when she heard the sound of something heavy landing on living room floor. *Shit, gotta call the police.* She reached for her phone, but it was no longer where she left it. *Someone's in the house.* Another loud crash followed.

"Hello? Is anyone here?" *I need another plan.* Cindy backed up to the block where the butcher knives were sheathed. Both of her hands trembled as she fumbled trying to remove one of the sharp objects. *I wish Mark was here.* Cindy placed both hands at the base of the weapon and started to inch her way towards the living room.

"My husband is coming home, so *you* better leave." Cindy stared into the darkness, grabbing the knife tighter. She reached the edge of the living room and raised her voice even louder. "I don't want any trouble...just leave!"

Cindy removed one hand from the blade, reaching out in search for the light switch. She ran her hand along the inside of the wall until her fingers felt the smooth surface of the panel. *Thank God.* Cindy didn't hesitate flipping them all, which abruptly engulfed the room with light. She put the other hand back onto the knife, prepared to strike out at *whoever* came into her line of vision. After scanning the spacious area, she realized what was responsible for causing the unexplained sound. *I really must have slammed the door hard.*

She loosened her grip on the knife, placing it down on the mantle above the fireplace. Cindy bent over and picked up a large wood carving resembling the body of a Saber-tooth Tiger. Satisfied there was no damage, she placed it back on the mantle. *I'm just being paranoid.*

Cindy walked back into the kitchen and grabbed a bottle of wine from the rack. *This should calm my nerves.* She poured herself a goblet full and headed up the stairs. *Time for some relaxation.* At her bedroom door, she began to shed her clothes. She stood in front of the mirrored closet for several minutes, obsessing about the usual physical imperfections as a woman in her late forties was known to do.

Cindy finished off her drink, exiting in the direction of the master bath. After pulling open the ivory curtain, she turned on the water. *Time for a little more wine.* Cindy rushed down the stairs, grabbing the bottle from the table.

On her way back up, she realized she couldn't hear the water running. *What the fuck?* Cindy stopped at the top of the stairs. Was Mark here and playing games with her?

"Mark, you asshole, is that you?" Bravery set in as she stormed the master bath. *Nothing. What's going on?*

"Hey, Mark, if you're here, I'm going to kick your ass."

By entering the bathroom, Cindy cut out any opportunity for escape. The dark, masked figure slipped out from her bedroom and was just a few feet from the bathroom doorway, hidden in the shadows.

Cindy restarted her bath and turned to walk out, but the man made his presence known as his large frame filled the doorway. His sudden appearance startled Cindy as she back peddled, losing her balance and falling. A scream erupted from the woman when her shoulder caught the edge of the porcelain toilet. Instantly, the man was on top of her. She tried to fend him off, but his gloved hand clasped around her throat and quickly closed her airway. Although she was losing consciousness, she was still able to see the silver-edged blade as it flashed high above her.

Cindy tried to lift herself off the ground, but it was all in vain. The next thing she felt was the sharpness of the steel as it penetrated her naked flesh.

"Ah!" she screamed, trying to push the intruder off.

Her feet lifted off the ground in an attempt to kick, but before she could get enough strength to deliver a blow, another throbbing sensation coursed through her. This time, she saw the blood flow from her. Cindy tried to bring her hands up but was too weak, and her arms just flailed aimlessly.

The last sensation Cindy Palentine felt was the knife as it left a deep trail along her jugular, ending all of her future hopes or dreams.

CHAPTER NINE

Patrick Morgan was sitting in the living room, detangling Christmas lights with five-year-old Kelsey when his wife entered the room. The disappointed look on Coral Morgan's face said it all. She held the cordless out to him. *Shit, family time over,* he thought.

"Pat, it's *your* boss."

Patrick shook his head, taking it from her. "Yes, sir."

"Morgan, cancel your day off. We got another dead woman. South side, 2111 Cedar Street. Meet me there in twenty."

Patrick walked to the kitchen, rubbing his forehead. "Is it Jamie Brooks?"

"No, some woman named Tamara Bowers...seems she's been missing from work for a few days. One of the other employees stopped by to check on her and discovered the body."

"Same method?"

"Let's put it this way...the girl who found her had to be given a sedative."

Fuck. "I'm on the way." Patrick put the phone back in the cradle.

Coral intercepted him in the kitchen as he was leaving. "Not tonight, Pat. Kelsey *really* needs you. She has been sleeping all day, just hoping to stay up and do the tree together. She's getting worse—"

"What do you mean worse?"

"Twice today she told me it was hard to breathe."

Patrick shook his head. "Did you call Dr. Simons?"

Coral touched him on the arm. "He wants us to bring her to the Children's Hospital early next week."

Patrick clipped his badge onto his belt. "For surgery?"

"He mentioned a few tests need to be done, but it sounds like it."

"I thought they wanted to wait until she was six."

Coral leaned her head on his chest. "I'm sorry...this is *my* fault—"

He wrapped his arms around her. "No, I won't let you do that. We knew the risk, and we decided to try again."

"If I was healthier, *maybe* the miscarriages wouldn't have happened, and Kelsey wouldn't have to pay for my selfishness."

Not your fault. God did this to us. Patrick felt the anger seep into his face, so he closed his eyes. "I need to go...let's talk about this tomorrow. It's probably going to be a long night...don't wait up." Patrick kissed her on the cheek.

Coral smiled. "Please be careful. We need you around here. Kelsey needs you now...more than ever."

Patrick peeked into the next room. His daughter sat on the floor, piecing together a nativity set. *I'll never understand how people can have confidence in something they can't see.*

"Coral, I gotta go." He then walked over and kissed his daughter on the head before he hurried out the door.

* * *

Patrick stopped at the yellow crime scene tape. The patrol officer manning the area recognized him and allowed him to pass through the front door. The smell of vanilla incense hit him with full force, and he followed it, leading him to a set of double doors. They appeared to be held open by thick bands of the familiar barbwire used on the first victim. *Definitely same guy.*

Patrick's view into the room was limited as several uniformed officers were amassed directly in the center. Cromartie was the focal point of the crowd, barking orders at one of the young evidence techs. Patrick was almost blinded by the onslaught of white flashes coming from the various cameras.

Cromartie noticed Patrick had arrived and motioned towards him. "Morgan, take a look at this," he bellowed.

Patrick forced his way through the crowd, finally reaching his boss. He looked down in horror. The crime scene was almost an exact replica of the previous murder, including the table in front of the victim. The surface was streaked with blood, and a butcher knife was again left in the center of the table.

Cromartie stared at him. "Tamara Bowers, thirty-six years old and recently divorced. Her ex lives in Des Moines. The local PD there will be keeping an eye out for us."

He didn't do this, Patrick thought. "Uh, huh. Doesn't hurt to look at him."

Cromartie ignored him. "This sicko followed the pattern…like the first one. Even down to the candles. However, the barbwire holding that door open *is* different."

Patrick kneeled down next to the bloodied woman. "Looks like he wanted to show off."

"Yeah, the wounds are in the same place." Cromartie pointed at the woman's feet and the steel protruding from them.

"But take a look right here."

Cromartie leaned in. "What?"

Patrick slipped on latex gloves and picked up the black candles, one at a time. "*All* of these are almost down to the wick. The others at the first crime scene were practically new."

Cromartie picked one up. "So, we can establish some time pattern on when the murders occurred…good thinking."

"Just an observation…I could be wrong." *Not really. This guy seemed to be a creature of habit.*

Cromartie clapped a hand on his shoulder. "Good observation."

Patrick shifted his position, inspecting the barbwire handcuffs. "See where her hands are tied and how the barbwire is wrapped? This would take time…*lots* of time."

Cromartie nodded. "The door was left unlocked, but no signs of forced entry besides that."

"She may have known her killer." Patrick stared into the woman's lifeless eyes.

Cromartie pointed to a middle-aged patrol officer. "Simpson, go check with your officers, and see if they found any other people who may have known this woman."

"Roger that, sir. I will canvass the area and let you know."

Patrick stood up, reaching for the butcher knife. "Just threw it on the table...not even worried about taking it with him."

"Maybe he left a print on this one." Cromartie handed him a paper bag.

I don't think so...not gonna be that easy. Patrick closed the bag. "Who found her?"

Cromartie pulled a notebook from his jacket. He thumbed through until he found the page he wanted. "Melanie Oliver. She and Bowers worked at the chain bookstore...Pinkerton's."

"Pretty upscale bookstore," Patrick noted.

Cromartie shook his head. "Never been. Well, Oliver told officers that the victim hasn't been at work for three days."

"Hmm. Is Ms. Oliver around here somewhere?"

"Actually, she is. We called an ambulance for her...appeared to be in shock at what she found. EMTs gave her something to calm her down."

Who wouldn't need something after that? "I think the quicker we talk to her, the better."

"If she isn't totally drugged out." Cromartie unclipped his portable radio. He pushed down on the transmitter. "Officer Alexander, how is our witness doing?"

The radio squelched. "Commander, she appears to be doing a *lot* better. Do you need her up there?"

Cromartie clicked the button. "No, we will be there in a while."

"10-4, sir," Officer Alexander responded.

A few minutes later, Patrick and Cromartie went to meet the witness at the back of the building. Officer Alexander stood at the back steps. Melanie Oliver, a young woman, maybe all of twenty, was clutching the officer's coat. She was not overly attractive, and her jet black hair appeared to have flecks of glitter in it.

Patrick smiled. "Hi, I'm Detective Morgan, and this is Commander Cromartie. I know you answered some questions for the other officer here, but I just have a few—"

Tears started to stream down her face. "Tamara's feet were nailed to the fucking floor. I've *never* seen anything that bloody."

Neither have I, until last week. "Melanie, how did Tamara get along with other people at work?"

"I guess ok...she was pretty cool to hang out with." She wrung her hands. "I was just coming here to check on her. Don't understand it, though..."

"What do you mean?

"Well, her Durango is parked at the bookstore. Weird she left it there."

Very weird, Patrick thought. He jotted it down in his notebook.

"Did you guys hang out at all?" Patrick asked.

Melanie bit her fingernails. "Sort of. We got drunk...if that's what you mean about hanging out."

"That's what I mean. A lot of people get drunk with you two?"

"Nah, some of the guys thought she was too flirty for being old, you know?"

If thirty-six is old, I'm in trouble. Patrick grinned. "So, none of the guys liked her flirting with them?"

She looked down. "Don't think so. She *did* have a guy who stared at her a lot, though."

Patrick cocked his head. "A boyfriend?"

"No, not a boyfriend...you know she was married once?"

"Yes, old people sometimes get married." Patrick chuckled. "So, no boyfriend, but someone came to visit her?"

Melanie scratched her head. "I'm not sure, but there was a guy who would watch her when she was in the store."

Maybe something here. "Did she ever talk to this gentleman?"

"I don't know for sure." Melanie shrugged. "There was one thing about him I'll *never* forget."

Patrick exchanged looks with Cromartie. "What was that?"

"He was sort of strange looking."

"Strange?"

"Yeah, this dude, his skin was the color of snow…maybe not that white but weird."

That can't be a coincidence. "Do you mean albino?"

"Is that what they call it? Yes, albino sounds right."

Serena Owens had first mentioned the man she saw had the strange color of skin; now, it was Melanie Brooks who saw possibly the same person. "Melanie, this is very important. Have you seen this man since Tamara's been gone?"

"No…not that I remember."

"You're pretty sure he hasn't been around?"

"Detective, I would remember his face anywhere. I haven't seen him around at all."

She would remember that face, I'm sure of it. Patrick stood up. "Melanie, would you be able to sit down with a sketch artist and give him a description?"

She bit more fiercely on her nails. "I can try…not promising anything, but I'll try for you."

Patrick touched her shoulder. "Great. Anything you can do is appreciated. I'll get it set up." Patrick stood up and waved for Cromartie to follow.

"I think we may have something." Patrick showed him the notes from the interview with Serena.

"Sounds like more than a fucking coincidence." Cromartie handed him back the green notebook.

Patrick pocketed it. "I'll check with Pinkerton's other staff and see if the store caught him on video."

"Good idea; keep me updated. I'll drive her down to the station so we can get the sketch guy on it." Cromartie started to walk away but turned around. "One more thing she said that's giving me the fucking willies. The woman's Durango is parked at the bookstore. My question is why?"

No goddamn way. Patrick's face turned white. "Someone gave her a ride home."

"And that someone sounds like it might be the albino." Comartie pointed at him.

Makes sense, Patrick thought. "You think he did something to the car?"

"Would it surprise you?"

Patrick shook his head. "At this point, nothing would surprise me...nothing at all."

CHAPTER TEN

Brandon Thornley stared out the window, admiring the falling snow as it blanketed his backyard. This was his favorite time of year, not because of the holidays, as one would think. No, it was something *else*. The arrival of winter, to him, was a cleansing of the entire year, as it completed a mysterious cycle. *Mysterious...like me*. Raising the window, he was immediately accosted by the frigid air.

He stood there for quite some time until he was interrupted by the chiming sound of his computer, knowing it was an alert from *Konnect2u*. *Excellent...more people to choose from*. Brandon sat down in front of the monitor in anticipation of finding someone new to satisfy his surging hunger. The screen popped up, showing several profile pictures. He tapped the mouse and scrolled through the information, deleting several of the requests without giving them fair consideration. *Not interesting enough for me*. When he was done, only two names remained for contention in his deadly game.

Melody Slavine was a dark-haired nineteen-year-old gothic artist, and for her age, she was actually quite famous. Brandon recognized several of the designs on her profile, as they corresponded with some of the wall prints hanging in the hallways of Langston Security Solutions. *Very fitting*.

The other name he had interest in was Collin Glover. The bald, stout fifty-year-old was a local attorney who specialized in ambulance chasing. If there was a major accident of any type involving injured persons, Collin was at the hospital, handing out his card to anyone within ten feet. *If anyone deserves to die, it's this guy*. Brandon printed out the profile information for both, then minimized the screen. Opening another browser window, he checked his e-mail. He deleted one message at a time until he stopped at one in particular.

Outstanding. Brandon clicked on the link, opening it. A separate window appeared. He typed in his user name and password. A few seconds later, Brandon was staring at the administrator page for Langston Security Solutions. He scanned the numerous menus, clicking on the correct tab. A list of highlighted names replaced the previous screen. Brandon worked his way through each, stopping at one that seemed familiar. *I know him.*

He moved the cursor to the minimized window and studied his friends list. *This is the guy.* Brandon browsed the photo section of the profile, but the only one available was a framed snapshot of an older model tan Chevrolet Caprice. *Likes his privacy.* He hit the button to take him to the *information about you* section of the profile and found the paragraph he wanted.

Brandon switched back to the list of names, quickly finding the contact information for the man. He picked up his desk phone and dialed.

A groggy voiced answered. "Donovan Petrie speaking."

"Mr. Petrie, this is Brandon Thornley from Langston Security Solutions. How are you this morning?"

"Hello, Mr. Thornley. I'm doing great! Just a little tired from a late night."

Brandon laughed. "We *all* have those. Say, the reason I'm calling you is this…we are down a few positions in the Security Department, and I reviewed your online application. I wanted to see if you could come for a personal interview?"

"Sir, the answer is yes. When do you want me there?"

Brandon glanced at his watch. "Meet me at the downtown office at three o' clock this afternoon."

"You got it, sir. I really appreciate the opportunity."

"No worries, Donovan…can I call you Donovan?"

Donovan laughed. "Of course. I haven't been in the industry for a few years…sort of got *sidetracked*."

"Well, I went over your scenario-based questions, and I like what I see. Now, let's save a few things for our meeting, okay?" *Best candidate on paper.*

Donovan hesitated. "Of course. It would be an honor to work for you."

"Don't be late then…and we'll see how everything goes."

Donovan chuckled. "No way will I be late."

"Excellent. See you then, Donovan." Brandon placed the receiver in the cradle. *Now, back to other pressing matters.*

He took the photocopies of Melody Slavine and Collin Glover and placed them side by side. Brandon gazed at the two for a considerable amount of time until he had them engraved into his memory. Normally, he would just decide, but today, it was time for *something* a little different. He stood up from the chair, opened the door, and walked down the hall, where his wife was still sleeping. Her long, brown hair was spilling out from underneath the sheets. *So beautiful.*

He sat on the edge of the bed, kissing her on the neck. "Carina, time to get up…don't want you late for your meeting."

Carina giggled. "Hey, you. Why in heaven are you up already?"

Brandon unrolled her blanket, exposing the black chemise, then lowered his head. "Sorry about last night…had a lot of work to do."

Carina yawned, then rubbed his face. "My dear, you can make it up to me…now."

Not what I had planned. "Tell you what, if you'll help me with something first, I'm all yours."

Carina sighed. "Hmm, you need my help? *That's* a first."

"Ouch. Yes…I *do*."

She shrugged. "Okay, but after…you are mine, Brandon Gregory Thornley."

Brandon crossed his heart. "Promise."

She got up, and he led her into his private office. "Okay, I have a little dilemma."

Carina smiled. "*You* have a dilemma? We better hurry to the doctor and get you checked out."

Brandon ignored her. "No, I have two people who I can do a blog on but can't decide."

"Really?" Carina raised an eyebrow.

Brandon nodded. "Yeah, the first is, Melody Slavine." He handed her the photocopy.

Carina tapped the picture. "Oh, she is the young artist who has all the god-awful billboards throughout town."

Not looking good, Melody. Brandon handed her the second photo. "What about this one?"

Carina's face turned red. "Wretched bastard, he cost the hospital over a million dollars for a slip and fall. We lost several staff due to that bugger."

Uh-oh, Collin. "I knew he was an attorney. Wasn't aware you had any dealings with him."

"Most hideous creature, that one." She flipped Collin Glover's photo on the desk. Carina regained her composure. "What's the blog about, anyway?"

Brandon quickly came up with something. "Well, the topic is personal security for local people in the media."

"Use that man...he would need an entire police force to keep him safe."

That wouldn't even be enough to stop me. Brandon laughed. "I guess it's settled then. Collin is the man."

Carina grabbed his hand. "Speaking of someone being the *man*...I think you owe me something."

Brandon sheepishly smiled. "Give me a few minutes...and I'll meet you in the bedroom."

"Oh, I don't think so. Now, mister."

"Okay, you're right...this other work will wait until later."

He followed her, his mind somewhere else. *Collin Glover, step up: you're the next contestant in my game of death.*

CHAPTER ELEVEN

Donovan Petrie entered through the glass doors and grabbed a cart from the rack. He had only gotten a few feet into the discount store when a gray-haired man dressed in an orange vest hurried towards him.

"Happy holidays. Do you need any help, sir?"

Don't have time for this. Donovan forced a smile. "Um, no, I just need a few things."

"You sure?" The man reached in his vest pocket and handed him a candy cane.

"Thanks, but I don't eat candy." Donovan gritted his teeth. "I'm fine; others may need you, though." He pointed at a young woman with two small children. He handed the red and white striped treat back to the man. "Give *this* to one of them."

The man nodded, making a beeline for the other customer.

Donovan pushed the cart through several aisles, grabbing the occasional grocery item as he tried to fit in with other shoppers. However, once he made a turn into the house wares section, his obsession overtook him.

The display was filled with knives of all sizes. *This is what I came for*. Donovan gazed at several and was lost in thought when he felt a tap on his shoulder.

"Sir, are you looking for something in particular?"

Donovan turned, facing the employee. *Fucking nice*. The girl was maybe in her late teens or early twenties, and her body was nearly perfect. The tan polo pulled tight against her breasts, barely allowing the lower button to fasten. The dark khaki shorts showed off her well-defined legs, causing Donovan to get excited.

He stared at her gold nametag. "Hi, Amanda. Just looking to find a nice gift for the relatives."

She caught him looking at her chest but ignored it. "I know we just got box set of these ones *here*." She pulled a knife from the shelf and handed it to him. "Very good quality and they have a lifetime warranty."

I could kill her with one stroke. "Wow, it feels pretty light, too." He held the blade with both hands.

She folded her arms. "I know…you want me to go grab a box from the warehouse?"

"How many come in a set?"

"Ten, usually. You probably don't need any more. I wouldn't think." She grinned.

Never can have enough. Donovan inspected the steel. "No, ten is *just* right." He put the knife into his cart. "I'll even get one for myself. Amanda, I think you have yourself a sale. Would you take them to the front, and I'll pick them up? I need a few more items." *Nails, electrical tape, and frozen pizza.*

"Sure, give me like five minutes."

"Okay, thank you again, *Amanda*."

Her smile faded. "Um, no problem…glad I could help." She rushed from the aisle.

Donovan reached up and grabbed two more of the blades. *Now I have what I need.* He pushed the cart through several more aisles and found the electrical tape and heavy duty nails. Donovan made his way to the checkout lane and was putting his purchases on the conveyor belt when he realized something was missing. *Shit.* He piled everything back in the cart and waved for the next person in line to take his place.

A few minutes later, he was standing in front of the frozen food section, searching the shelves for his favorite snack. *Supreme with extra cheese. Can't beat that.* Donovan turned to his cart but was distracted by a two loud voices: a man and a woman. They were on the opposite side of the aisle, but their anger was noticed by other customers as they hurried by. The man was over six feet tall with mid-shoulder blond hair. He was covered in dark leather and a cast covered his right arm. The focus of his anger was a petite woman with brown hair. She was dressed in the same fashion, but her tough exterior appeared to be a façade. She was backed up against another refrigeration unit and appeared to be crying.

He's not very nice. Donovan slowed his cart, stopping just a few feet from the two.

The man whirled around. "What the fuck do *you* want?"

Temper, temper. Donovan pointed. "Just need to get some frozen onion rings and a pizza."

"We're having a conversation…can you come back?" The man glared.

Donovan shook his head, pointing to his watch. "Not really; I have somewhere to be."

The man's eyes narrowed as he stepped aside. "Fine, get your goddamn shit then."

"Thanks." He picked up the two items, tossing them in the cart.

The man kept staring at him but said nothing as Donovan walked away. He was almost to the check out counter when he noticed a uniformed police officer standing near a soda machine. The hairs on his neck began to tingle, and his mouth suddenly became dry. *Relax.*

Regaining his composure, he approached the officer. *I can't pass this up.* Donovan smiled. "Sir, I think there might be something going on by the frozen food section."

The officer seemed young, and the idea of something happening in his jurisdiction put him on alert.

"Sir, what do you mean *something*?"

Be convincing. Donovan moved closer. "Looks like maybe a *domestic violence* situation."

The officer frowned. "You got a description for me?" He pulled out a notepad.

Of course. "A man and woman, dressed in black leather. He's got blond hair past his collar. She *really* looked upset."

"Okay, thanks for letting me know. I'll check it out." The officer hurried away.

Now the fun begins. Donovan paid for his items and headed to his car. After putting everything in the trunk, Donovan sat down behind the wheel and waited. A few minutes later, the officer appeared with the man and woman trailing behind. The officer spoke to them for a few minutes, then turned and left the area. The blond man looked enraged as he stared out into the parking lot, looking for his accuser. They stopped a few rows from him, getting into a late-model yellow Mustang. The car screeched out of the lot, with Donovan following from a safe distance.

Several miles later, the Mustang turned into a residential street cluttered with broken-down vehicles and tipped over garbage cans. *Nice neighborhood,* Donovan thought. They continued down the block until finally stopping in front of an ancient two story. The paint appeared to be chipped away on most of the exterior, and the glass from all the windows had been replaced with slabs of wood. *Shouldn't be too difficult to break in there.*

Donovan turned off the engine and watched as the two exited the vehicle, apparently engaged in another argument. When he felt it was safe, he drove by the Mustang, scribbling the license plate information on an unused napkin. Donovan quickly checked out the surrounding house, making several mental notes. He smiled to himself. *Sometimes easy prey just drops right in your lap.*

CHAPTER TWELVE

Patrick Morgan sorted through the stacks of folders on his desk in search of the file on Justus Alleandro. *Poor Justus...horrible way to go.* The Davenport Police didn't hesitate to overnight the much needed information, especially since Commander Cromartie mentioned the killer had struck here twice. Patrick was almost finished with the pile when something sailed through the air from behind and landed right in front of him.

"Hey!" He turned.

Commander Cromartie stood there, arms crossed. "I went through this *whole* fucking file...take a look, and tell me what you think."

Patrick flipped open the folder. "I'll give you a heads up if I find something."

"Just got a call. I gotta meeting with the Chief and the media. Call the cell if you find anything at all."

Media? Not good. "Good luck with that. You plan to mention *all* the details of the crime scene to them?"

Cromartie buttoned his coat. "Not if we don't have to...pray we don't."

Patrick shook his head. "No thanks."

"Oh, I forgot...that's not your thing." Cromartie snickered.

No, it really wasn't. "I'm a fact guy...you should know by now."

Cromartie leaned over him, pointing to the color photos of Justus Alleandro. "I sure as hell hope *he* believed in something. See you later." He walked out of the office.

Patrick grabbed one of the photographs. Justus Alleandro apparently was taking a shower when the killer found him.

Different this time. His arms were extended over his head, and he was fastened in place to the light blue shower wall by two sets of industrial-sized nails. One was on the top of the feet. The trademark signature of this killer. The other was where both hands met as they were extended. *One nail piercing two hands. Where was the barbwire?* Patrick unclipped the narrative from the other side of the folder, scouring it, in search of the witness list.

Nothing at all. The statement of the first officer on scene reported an unknown caller had left an anonymous tip about the body. *How convenient.* Patrick flipped through the other pages, looking for the call logs from the dispatch center. *Not a fucking thing here. Cromartie didn't go through the whole log, or he would have noticed it.*

Patrick jumped up and headed for Cromartie's office. *Shit.* He thought about turning around when he saw the gray-haired Margie Stapleton sitting at her desk. She was Cromartie's administrative assistant, but to the Commander, she was *much* more than that. Patrick remembered the night he had to pick up a prescription for Kelsey and stopped at the station to check on a case he was working. He accidentally walked in on the two as they were engaged in the highest level of *quid pro quo.* The two tried to play it off, but ever since then, Margie would hardly speak with Patrick.

He stopped in front of her, holding up the file. "Hey, Margie, can you tell me if there are more pages to this file?"

Margie adjusted her glasses as she kept typing. "*Detective,* what you have there is what came in this morning."

Always makes me feel like I'm a child. "Well, I wasn't sure...couldn't find any dispatcher logs—"

She stopped typing. "Then *they* didn't send any." Margie looked up and resumed with the keyboard.

Maybe another approach. "You know, I *never* said a word about you and the Commander. It's not my business. I would, however, *really* appreciate it if you could check for a cover letter." He smiled.

Margie removed her glasses, placing them on the table. "The package came right to him this morning." She stood up and opened the door to Cromartie's office. A few minutes later, she returned, handing him a piece of paper. "I think *this* might be what you are looking for."

No doubt knowledge is power. Patrick nodded. "Thanks. I'll get it back to you."

"Patrick, this is big case for him." Margie lowered her head.

"It is for *all* of us." Patrick walked back to his desk. He scrolled down the paper and located the Davenport's Police point of contact.

Sgt. Scott Milburn
Davenport Police
319-999-0001

Patrick dialed the number. A few rings later, a young woman answered. "Davenport Police, Jessica speaking."

"Hello, this is New Haven Police Detective Patrick Morgan. I'm looking for Sergeant Milburn."

"Hold, please."

The woman's voice was replaced with the sound of holiday music. *Just a little early.* Patrick was waiting several minutes, humming along with the melody, when he heard a strong male voice answer.

"Good afternoon, Detective Morgan. What can I help you with?"

"Sergeant, I was going over the file you sent, and some of the paperwork seems to be missing."

"What's missing?"

"The call log from the dispatch center."

"Hmm, I thought it was in the packet…you sure?"

"Yes, I went through everything. It's not here."

"Shit, did you get the officer's narrative?"

Patrick pulled out the report. "Yeah, right here in my hand, dated for 11-09-09, at 2300."

"Good, Patrick. Been trying to find anyone who happened to be in the area during the murders."

"Find anything so far?" Patrick asked.

"Nothing other than what I sent up to you guys. Hold on...I was gone the last couple of days. Looks like someone put a few files in my inbox."

Could be something. "Sure, I'll hold on." Patrick could hear the sound of papers being shuffled.

"Patrick, you're not gonna fucking believe this."

Try me. "What?"

"I'm looking at a supplemental report from another officer called back to the scene just two days ago."

"Supplemental?" *Only used when something needs to be added, maybe a witness.*

"Yes, let me scan through it for a minute."

"See if there's anything that mentions a tan or beige Caprice." Patrick chewed on his fingernails. *It's gotta be him.*

"Beige Caprice?"

"Scott, the car was witnessed at two locations in town. One involving a murder, the other a missing person's case." *Soon to be another dead body.*

A short pause ensued. "Fuck me, our witness statement mentions it...this is our guy."

Yes. Patrick slammed his fist on the desk. "Any plate information?"

"Can't seem to find any, but I'll go talk to this guy myself, just to make sure."

"Is there any way you would be able to fax me the report so I can take a peek?"

"Of course. I'll send it ASAP."

Patrick loosened his tie. "Great. Let me know if anything pans out with your witness."

"Gotcha. Let me get moving on this, and I'll keep you posted."

Patrick opened his notebook and turned to the page with the vehicle description. "If I find out something on my end, I'll give you a call, as well."

"10-4. I hope you get this son-of-a-bitch before he does it again."

"Scott, so do I." Patrick hung up, staring at the photos of Justus Alleandro. He made a few notes and closed the folder. Patrick was about to call Commander Cromartie when his portable radio exploded with activity.

"Dispatch to Detective Morgan," the voice squelched.

Patrick grabbed the radio. "Go ahead with your transmission, dispatch."

"Sir, I need you to respond to United Ministries on 1229 Euclid for a Homicide."

A church? Now that *was fucked up.* "10-4, dispatch. Better give a heads up to the Commander and get him rolling."

"Sir, officer on scene indicates it looks like the missing Jamie Brooks."

Shit, too late to save her. "10-4, dispatch. I'm *en route.*"

"Roger that, sir." the radio went silent.

Patrick grabbed his coat and bolted out of the office. The bodies of New Haven's citizens were piling up, and without identifying the driver of the Caprice, there was no telling how many more would be added.

CHAPTER THIRTEEN

Donovan stopped in front of the immense structure and admired the mirrored glass, which covered the entire building. *Expensive.* He continued inside to the entrance, which was manned by two well-dressed security personnel. One of them gave him a most disapproving stare. The bald-headed goliath snickered, motioning for their guest to come forward. Donovan took off his suit jacket, dress belt, and removed a handful of loose change from his front pocket. He placed it on the conveyor belt of the x-ray machine, stepping through the magnetometer. The quiet hum of the device signaled he was cleared to enter further into the facility for his interview with Brandon Thornley. One of the guards handed him a map, circling his destination.

Show time. Donovan followed the directions, maneuvering the winding hallways. Several people did a double-take as they passed by. *Simple-minded fucks.* He stopped in front of a bank of glass elevators and pushed the button. Donovan was about to step in when he felt a tap on his shoulder. A husky, middle-age man in a dark uniform grinned at him.

"Sir, excuse me. Are you Donovan Petrie?"

Hmm, welcoming committee...nice. "Yes, and you are..."

The man extended his hand. "Monty York. Boss sent me to meet you."

The man wasn't even fazed by my appearance. Donovan cocked his head. "Already keeping tabs on me?"

Monty laughed. "Mr. Thornley knows what's going on *everywhere* in this building."

Probably doesn't know I'm going to kill him. "Well, that would be a good thing."

"Just think of Mr. Thornley as a high paid Santa Claus…knows when you have been naughty or nice."

Definitely naughty this year. "I'll have to remember that."

Monty ushered him onto the elevator. The man took a key from his ring and inserted it into a lock on the elevator panel. He noticed Donovan was starting at him. "Nobody can get to the administration offices unless they have this."

And if everything goes right, I will. "Tight security."

Monty clipped the ring back onto his belt. "That's how the boss likes it."

The elevator doors opened, and Monty escorted him through a maze of corridors, passing large offices at every turn. They finally stopped in front of a set of double doors. There were no markings on the nameplate, and in all actuality, the entrance looked very ordinary compared to everything else Donovan had seen. Monty led him inside, and to the right was another interior door surrounded by Plexiglas. *Now, this is what I expected.* Monty knocked twice before they walked in.

Donovan glanced around the room, noticing only a few pieces of furniture. The room's real attractions were the countless die-cast action figures scattered throughout and framed movie posters that covered all four walls. *The guy likes sci-fi.* Donovan raised an eyebrow at his tour guide as Brandon Thornley studied several folders on his desk.

He looked up, smiling at his visitors. "Monty, thanks for bringing Mr. Petrie up. I'll let you know when we're done."

"Yes, boss." Monty exited.

Brandon Thornley pushed himself away from the desk. Donovan was surprised at how chiseled the Security Director was. *Stronger and larger than me.* Brandon stood up and reached for the hand of his visitor. The sheer force of the man's grasp almost caused Donovan to grimace.

Brandon smiled. "Glad you could make it today."

"Thank you, sir. Been a while since I've done this sort of work."

"No worries. We can put you right back into the thick of things." Brandon motioned for him to sit.

Donovan grinned. "Sir, I have been doing something totally different the last few years."

Brandon reached into his sports coat and pulled out two cigars. "*De Lase*, my favorite. May I offer you one?"

Donovan fingered the fine import. "Been a while for that, too."

"Ha! Then, Mr. Petrie, it's definitely time." Brandon reached over and grabbed a silver lighter. Donovan noticed it was monogrammed with the letters GT. *I know those initials.* "So, what have you been doing? The online application just says private contractor."

Just fucking killing people. Donovan puffed on the cigar. "Mr. Thornley, I have been involved mostly in construction stuff...using my hands to create things has been my latest passion."

Brandon nodded. "I admire you for that...leaving a possibly profitable career to follow your heart."

Donovan sighed. "It's been exciting, but with the economy the way it's been, I figured it would be best to get back into my field."

"Well, Mr. Petrie, I'm extremely glad you thought of us. I usually scour the database a few times a week for viable candidates, and man, it was a blessing to see someone with your skills on the market."

This guy is actually digging me...that's fucking weird. "Well, I'll tell you something funny...or, maybe I shouldn't—"

"Don't leave me hanging now, Mr. Petrie."

Should I tell him? Donovan took another puff. "Okay, I joined this social networking site and saw your name on there."

Brandon cocked his head. "*Konnect2u*, right?"

Dead right. "That's it. I read your profile and decided to send you a friend request."

Brandon rubbed his chin. "The snake design with a heart...very intriguing style you have."

Donovan shook his head. "Thanks. I like to *think* I have a unique style anyway. I check your posts daily, and it sort of got me thinking about the security field again."

"*Again*, lucky for us, Mr. Petrie." Brandon placed his cigar in a black glass ashtray. "Maybe I will have to advertise job openings on my page?" Brandon grinned. "That's truly *one* way for social networking to have an impact."

There will be another way. "I just think I'm ready to come back to this." Donovan finished his cigar.

Brandon eyed him, then grabbed a pen from his desk drawer. "If you're ready to get back in the groove, *we* need you here at Langston Security Solutions." He scribbled on a few pieces of paper and pushed the folder across the desk. "This is the packet I need filled out for security clearance and access. Once you're done, take this down to Jade in Human Resources on the first floor. She'll get everything you need: badge, photo identification, security code access, etc."

Donovan stood up. "Brandon, thanks for this."

"No need to thank me...just do a good job, Mr. Threat Assessment Analyst."

I intend to. "When do you want me back here?"

Brandon peered down at his desk calendar. "Monday. Is that enough time to finish any projects you have?"

"I only have one left...should have that knocked out by tomorrow." *More than enough time.*

"Excellent, Mr. Petrie, let me know. Don't hesitate to give me a call if you need anything."

"I will."

Monty York returned, escorting him to the first floor, then on to Human Resources. Donovan finished up with the HR office, then headed to his car in the parking garage. He studied the notepad on the passenger seat and thought about the abusive biker from Plaxton's Super Center. *One more kill left before I get to you, Mr. Thornley...just one more.*

CHAPTER FOURTEEN

United Ministries was once a thriving house of worship. Parishioners filled the seats and raised their voices to the heavens. Even the youth choir was paramount in contributing to the church's success. The yearly vocal competitions usually resulted in the addition of extra income to add to the organization, in the form of purchasing much-needed spiritual literature to hand out to the non-believers of New Haven.

Today, however, the crumbling structure was just a refuge for runaway pets and their occasional food source. Patrick Morgan was amazed that the members of the church let this great landmark of the city fall to the wayside. The former pastor of the church had spent his whole life building up the congregation, and after the man's sudden death, the church members started to dwindle in number, and the programs offered almost disintegrated overnight. Only a few hard-core followers remained, which forced the executive board to cease operations. This was the telltale result. *So is life and...apparently death.*

Patrick looped his shield around his neck as he exited the vehicle. The desolate neighborhood was now populated with scores of New Haven patrol units, and it even appeared that the local fire department had responded. *Hope we don't need them.* He had made it only a few steps when a newly academy-trained officer stopped him.

"Sir," he stammered.

Just a little nervous. Patrick glanced down at his nametag. "What's up, Officer Rhodes?"

The sandy haired man shook his head. "Looks like it's the missing girl."

"Jamie Brooks?"

He nodded. "Yes...but it wasn't easy. Some of the...um...local wildlife got to her, sir."

Dead and fucking eaten? "Officer Rhodes, is Commander Cromartie here?"

"Not yet, sir."

"Okay. Make sure we have the medical examiner on the way."

"Already been contacted."

"Good." Patrick pointed towards the building. "Is it safe up there?"

Officer Rhodes gave him a nervous smile. "Fire guys walked through...said they didn't *think* it would collapse."

"Wonderful." Patrick waved to him.

The ground surrounding the latest crime scene was thick with snow. Patrick trudged his way through, taking note of the lack of footprints along the way. Within a few minutes, he was inside, heading towards the second floor. There were officers still marking the scene with yellow tape when he arrived at the top of the landing. A police officer Patrick had known since starting at New Haven had tears streaming down his face. He pointed to the last door at the end of the hallway.

As Patrick approached the splintered entrance, the pungent odor of rotting flesh attacked his senses, causing his eyes to water. He choked back his urge to contaminate the crime scene as he moved into the interior room. The apartment was larger and in better shape than he expected. Patrick gawked at the living area, and even through all of the decay, could see this used to be *someone's* home.

A few yards to the right was a plain pine door, and Patrick could hear voices coming from behind. He eased it open and saw the room was barely larger than a walk-in closet. It had been converted into a makeshift kitchen with a coffee-stained table and broken microwave. Two plainclothes officers were standing around the nude body of a young girl snapping photographs.

That's her. Jamie Brook's blackened and decomposed body was on the opposite side of the table. She was wired to a metal chair that was *way* too small for her. Patrick noticed bite-sized chunks of flesh were missing throughout her body. *She didn't deserve this.* He moved in behind the victim. Most of the crime scene had been repeated except for the four dark candles. They were present, but the long broad wicks remained, which indicated that maybe the killer had been interrupted.

Patrick cleared his throat. "Who called this in?"

One of the plainclothes officers stopped taking pictures. He slightly turned his head. "Young kid. He was sledding or some shit and had to use the restroom."

Patrick cocked his head. "So he broke in?"

"It appears that way."

Patrick sighed. "Who is he…and where's he at now?"

"Fifteen-year-old Aiden Jacobs. He lives a few blocks from the church. He said *this* place has been quite busy the last week or so."

Not so abandoned. Patrick's eyes lit up. "Seriously?"

"Yeah." The officer thumbed over in the direction of his partner. "The kid told Steve and I that about once a day, *somebody* is wandering around here."

Somebody is our killer. "Can I speak with him?"

"We can't get in touch with either of the parents yet. Officer Wright is sitting in front of his house. The kid has a sister who can give us consent."

That's where I'm headed. "You find anything else?"

The officer pumped his fist. "Bet your ass we did. Check this out." The man walked over to the microwave. He reached up and withdrew a brown paper bag, then handed it to the detective.

Patrick gave him a questioning look before opening it. *Holy shit.* Patrick peered in, and was so overwhelmed with excitement that he almost spilled out the contents. "Where was *this* at?"

"Sort of strange…over there in the corner."

The fucking same place? "We need to get DNA off it ASAP." Patrick closed the bag. "I need the info on that boy. As of right now, he's the best lead we have."

The officer handed him a piece of paper. "Officer Wright is outside the house."

"Great, when Commander Cromartie gets here, tell him I went over to check on this."

"Sir, you think the boy saw something worthwhile?"

Patrick glared at the broken corpse of Jamie Brooks. "For *everyone's* sake, I fucking hope so."

* * *

Patrick squinted at the piece of yellow paper, as he finally found the address for Aiden Jacobs. The narrow alley wasn't cleared, and maneuvering the unmarked over fresh snow bordered on treacherous, even for an experienced driver like Patrick. He slid to a stop, just barely avoiding the parked patrol unit of Officer Wright. Patrick exited and stopped at the rear of Wright's vehicle. Officer Wright forced open the door.

The stout, pock-marked faced officer lifted himself out of the car, smiling at the investigator. "Hey, boss. The kid's sister just showed. I told her to wait inside until you got here."

"Great, did the boy say *anything* to you at all?"

Officer Wright adjusted his duty belt. "Nah, he looked pretty scared…was quiet as a goddamn church mouse all the way here."

Finding a mutilated dead girl will do that. "Hmm. Hopefully, he can give us something."

Patrick and Officer Wright made their way through the broken tree limbs and scattered garbage. The remains of a recently slaughtered deer was hanging on the rear of the porch. Patrick covered his face, shaking his head at Wright. The older man chuckled, as he pushed the carcass aside without the slightest hesitation.

Fucking nice. Patrick felt the sting of the frigid air whip around him. "No screens?"

"Guess that's on the makeover to-do list, huh?" Officer Wright blew into his gloveless hands. He tapped on the door, but there was no answer.

Patrick scowled. "You gotta be kidding."

Officer Wright shrugged. "Not surprising." He knocked again; this time, the door hinge shook with violently. Patrick could hear the sound of heavy footsteps coming from above. *About time.* The door creaked open. A blond boy, no older than his mid teens, was standing in the entryway. He was shirtless, and several scars covered his lanky midsection. Patrick grimaced. *Razor strap.*

"Mom and Dad aren't here. You cops?"

Patrick nodded. "We are."

The boy bit on his fingernails. "I'm a little scared. Don't want to get in trouble."

Patrick smiled. "We're not here to get you into trouble. I'm Detective Morgan, and that's Officer Wright. We just have a few questions for you, son."

Aiden Jacobs folded his arms. "Megan says I should tell you, but I don't want to get in trouble—"

"*Nobody's* in trouble...just want a little help from you." Patrick smiled.

"Help? I was so scared when I saw...the girl." He motioned them inside to a tiny living room. Most the furniture appeared to be second hand, and the only evidence of modern technology was a red and turquoise lava lamp. Aiden seemed to notice the reaction of the officers. "Dad doesn't like televisions or electronics of *any* kind. He thinks they rot your brain, and they are evil."

Okay, Dad's a nut job. "Well, I know you can't watch T.V. *all* the time." Patrick laughed.

Officer Wright scrunched his face in a disapproving manner, but he laughed as well.

"Yeah, he's probably right," Aiden whispered.

Patrick sat down on the stained couch. He pulled out the notebook. "Aiden, one of the officers mentioned you'd seen someone going in and out of the old church?"

"Sir, for the last few weeks, I have seen someone going behind the church into the graveyard. But in the last couple of days, I saw someone actually inside *there*." Aiden lifted a skinny finger and pointed towards the living room window.

A graveyard? Patrick jotted down the information. He exchanged a glance with Officer Wright. This was apparent news to him as well. Wright grabbed the cell phone from his belt and headed towards the kitchen.

"Aiden, did you get a good look at him?" Patrick asked.

The boy quickly looked away. "No, not too good."

Patrick *knew* the boy was scared. "Did he see *you*?"

"Not really…" Aiden stammered. "I think *maybe* I saw his face." He closed his eyes.

Patrick was on the edge of his seat. "Aiden, *come on*. Don't leave me hanging here."

The boy looked up. His pupils fixated on the window. "Pale…it was like the color of snow."

Not a fucking coincidence. "You ever see him before?"

"No, I would have remembered him." Aiden's body trembled.

Patrick moved closer and knelt beside him. "Hey, we are going to keep people around here. We won't let him hurt you."

"He looked dead…like a ghost."

He's gonna wish he was. "Did you see if he had a car?"

"He was walking. I don't think he drove."

Patrick scribbled down a few more notes. "So, you saw *him* go into the graveyard?"

Aiden's eyebrows narrowed. "Um, that wasn't him."

Patrick stopped writing. He cocked his head. "I thought *you* said someone was in the graveyard."

"I did…but that *wasn't* the same man. This guy was huge…and he was lugging a large bag."

What the fuck? Who was this guy? "Okay, you're sure?"

Aiden cringed. "Yeah, two different guys. Didn't really see his face, but man…he had a freaking sweet car."

"Really? What kind?"

"Not too sure of the model, but I can tell you it was a Mercedes," Aiden said in a matter-of-fact tone.

"*Mercedes?*"

"Yep. Saw that car in the new auto magazine at the gas station."

Officer Wright came back into the living room. A stern look on his face told Patrick this wasn't good news.

Patrick turned his attention back to Aiden. "Great, did you catch the plate info?"

Aiden shrugged. "Didn't have any...just a new dealer paper plate on the back."

"Remember what color?" Patrick smiled.

Aiden bit his lip for a few seconds before blurting it out. "Black and red."

Can't be too many dealerships in town with that combination. "Aiden, this really helps us get a start on things." Patrick patted him on the shoulder. "I'll give your parents a call later tonight. I'd like you to give our sketch artist the best description you can. Could you do that for me?"

Aiden's face turned white. "I guess I could."

Patrick gave him a warm smile. "Great. I know you're scared...but we'll be here. Officer Wright will keep extra patrols around the house."

Officer Wright smiled. "You're going to be okay, Aiden."

Aiden had stopped shivering and stared at Patrick. "Sir, do you think this guy will come after me?"

I hope not. "You don't need to worry...we'll protect you. You didn't get a great look at him...right?"

"No, just his weird face."

Enough for a sketch, at least. Patrick dropped a business card on the table. "If you remember anything else, give me a ring."

"Sure I will, sir." Aiden opened the door, escorting them out.

The two investigators walked to the edge of the driveway, staring at the crumbling church.

"Well, now were looking for two people, instead of one." Patrick zipped up his coat.

"I sent several officers to the area. So far, doesn't look promising. Too much white stuff covering all the headstones." Officer Wright tapped the snow from his boots.

"I'll do some checking on dealerships. If it was a recent purchase, shouldn't be too hard to track." Patrick flung open his car door. "You know, a second person on the abandoned property doesn't make sense."

"Unless the boy was wrong."

"There is *that* possibility." A grim look appeared on Patrick's face. "Hmm. Even though this place is dump, *someone* still has ownership."

"Patrick, I'm not positive, but I think the former pastor of this church still has some relatives in this area…a boy, possibly?"

Patrick shrugged. "I don't do church."

"Shit, I know who his son is. The name Brandon Thornley ring a bell?"

Patrick pulled up his collar. "The corporate security guru?"

Officer Wright nodded. "Yup, about fifteen years ago, a parishioner of the church found his father hanging from the church rafters."

"Sounds fucked up." *Really fucked up.*

"You think *that's* fucked up? They kept a few secrets out of the papers."

"About the suicide?"

"It *wasn't* a suicide." Officer Wright walked over to him.

"Someone hung him up there?" Patrick scratched his head.

Officer Wright nodded. "Crucified him…just like back in Biblical times. His hands were barb-wired behind his back, feet nailed to the rafter wood, and *something* was engraved in his forehead."

"Nailed and barb-wired? What are you talking about?" Patrick stopped brushing at the snow. "You sure?"

Officer Wright bit his lip. "Yeah, I couldn't tell you anything about what was carved into his flesh, but apparently, the police brass didn't want to release *any* of the details."

Wouldn't want to scare citizens. "Should be annotated in the police report."

Officer Wright turned to walk away. "Or so you would think?"

Patrick threw the ice scraper in the back seat. "I'm going to check in the archives. Do me a favor?"

"Sure."

"Keep this conversation between the two of us."

Officer Wright put a finger to his mouth. "Consider my lips to be sealed."

Patrick smiled. "Thanks, I'll keep you posted, if I find anything."

Officer Wright waved, pulling the patrol car from the alleyway. Patrick retreated inside his own vehicle, thinking, *Nails and barbwire were used on all of the victims, including the former pastor…fifteen years ago. This is hardly a coincidence.*

CHAPTER FIFTEEN

The Law Offices of Glover, Beston, and Stamner were situated in the heart of New Haven's ethnic melting pot. The simple, one-story brick structure resembled most of the others on the block, except for the thin metal sign above the entryway identifying the occupants. Collin Glover was the most senior of the trio, and his fixation with easy-to-win law suits made him the most approachable by prospective clients.

The stout, forty-something-year-old had a heavy addiction to the neighborhood drug of choice, and most others in his profession believed that alone had taken away his projected career running the gambit in corporate law. Most days, he needed to take a hit of methamphetamine just to get through, but *today* was different. Collin smiled as he opened the black folder. The jury had seen fit to award his client the amount he proposed. *That never happens*, he thought. He stared at the bank draft, and the urge for celebrating took over his body. *A few choice ladies are just what I need.*

He jumped from behind the desk and strutted over to a cracked wall mirror. The puffy bags underneath both eyes told him he was becoming old...*fast*. Collin straightened out his dark suit coat, trying to look the part of an established professional. He cracked the office door; his other associates were standing around the cappuccino maker. The two stopped chatting when they saw their partner emerge.

Collin gave them a fake smile. "Gentlemen, we did well today."

Rich Beston took a sip from his Styrofoam cup. The University of Dallengreen graduate and former collegiate athlete needed a place to get his feet wet. Collin had given him a chance to shine.

"Hey, moneybags, I know that means you're splurging on fine cuisine?"

Collin playfully punched him in the arm. "Hmm, you did a great job on the brief. How about a microwave burrito and a diet soda?"

Reginald Stamner, a Univeristy of Southern Nebraska alum and second year corn-fed associate, almost dropped his own cup. "Damn, not cool, Collin."

"I'm messing with you guys. I have something planned for tomorrow night for the three of us, but *right now*...I have something to take care of." Collin winked at the two.

Carl looked down at his watch. "It's still pretty early in the evening. You got a hot piece of ass lined up?"

Two, actually. Collin waved them off. "Nothing like that. I have to visit a potential client. I'll keep you both in the loop, if it pans out."

He eased out the door and headed down the rusty staircase. Collin turned up the street. The slick sidewalks made it difficult to walk, but his destination wasn't too far, and *his* reward would be far greater than this little annoyance. He crossed over to a side street, but the lack of lighting made him uneasy. *I don't like this.*

Collin slowly reached down and unzipped his briefcase. He fumbled through the interior with urgency until his hand was gripped around the nickel-plated object. The small caliber handgun was *just* a precaution, but Collin felt solace knowing he could act if one of the local neighborhood dwellers decided to attack. He eased the weapon into his coat pocket as he rushed across the final street and home to tonight's activities.

Ravine's Goldmine was the perfect getaway for people wanting to try their odds in the gambling world. The glass building looked more like an energy-saving residence than a state-of-the-art casino. Marveling at the overcrowded parking lot, he pushed his way through the double doors.

Collin gave an I'm-here-don't-fuck-with-me nod to the acne-ridden, pencil-necked security officer stationed in a small booth. The young man returned the gesture, motioning for Collin to walk to the elevator. A few seconds later, the door to the elevator opened. He removed his keycard and pushed a button on the panel. A minute later, he stepped out on the fourth floor onto a red-carpeted catwalk, high above slot machines, table games, and simulated racing monitors.

Collin followed the narrow path until it emptied out into a massive foyer. Several feet away, two heavy, dark-skinned males were standing guard over a series of closed doors. The bulges in their suit coats told Collin the owner was serious about protecting her business.

One of the men knocked on the door, and within a minute, a scantily clad Asian woman appeared and whispered to them. She turned and made eye contact with the attorney, almost causing him to erupt right where he was standing. The thin layer of satin was unable to hide her feminine attributes. She motioned for him to follow her, and Collin was eager with desire.

One of the men tapped him on the shoulder as he passed. He handed him a small clear baggie of white powder. Collin reached into his coat and stuffed a wad of bills into the man's hand. With a quick nod, Collin was behind closed doors and in a passionate embrace with the dark-haired beauty. *A fix and a fuck. What more can I ask for?*

* * *

Brandon Thornley had almost been discovered. The hooker-seeking drug user had turned around several times during the brisk walk to the casino. Once he had realized the destination of his prey, Brandon hurried back to his own car. He followed the directions he had printed off the Motor Vehicle Registration web site. Within fifteen minutes, he had set up temporary residence in a parking ramp across from Collin's condominium. A few police patrol units passed through the lot, but with the combination of frigid temps and lightly fallen snow, it would be difficult to tell if anyone inhabited the Mercedes. *You gotta love this weather.*

Brandon opened the middle console and removed a dark plastic case. He chose one of the metal devices and placed it inside his shirt pocket. He picked up his laptop and stared at the photo of the exterior lock of Collin Glover's residence. *I just love technology.* He shut down the operating system and stowed the laptop beneath the passenger seat.

Brandon peeked at his watch. *Eleven thirty. Just a few more hours.* He eased the driver's side door open and scanned the area for potential witnesses. When he was satisfied the area was secure, he scurried to the stairwell entrance, stopping at the foyer to the building's entrance. It wouldn't budge. *Fuck. This could be a quick trip.*

After a few seconds of staring at the door, he realized the door had no secondary access point or installed card reader. He again tried it; this time, it opened. The sound of scraping metal from the worn floor plate eased his tensions. *Temporarily frozen, I guess.* He walked through the maze of interior tunnels until locating the hallway that gave the killer access to the condominium's entryway. Within a few minutes, he was in front of Collin Glover's home. Brandon made quick work of the lock and slipped inside. The scent of cinnamon permeated the confines as he moved throughout. *Please, no surprises.*

He removed a compact light, searching one room at a time until he was satisfied the complex was empty. Then, he returned to the front of the house, stopping in front of a black and red oval table with matching chairs. From inside his coat, he removed several items, inspecting each, before placing them on the table. Brandon slumped down in one of the chairs, as he began to wait for Collin Glover to return. A glance of his watch quickened his pulse. A thin line of perspiration started to bead on his forehead. *Just a matter of time now...a matter of time.*

CHAPTER SIXTEEN

Collin Glover's sexual appetite had been satisfied, but the two women had *more* than convinced him their skills would be useful for the rest of the evening. Collin *did* have a preferred taste for Asian women, and after he supplied them with all the drugs and booze they wanted, they decided not to charge him for the extra time. *Free is always the choice.* The three walked back to the law firm, but Collin was sober enough to realize *that* wasn't the best idea. They piled into his Jaguar, and after a short ride, they pulled into a parking garage adjacent to his condo. The tires squealed as the car came to stop well outside the yellow parking lines. Collin reached down to pick up his briefcase, but a wet kiss on his neck made him start thinking with another part of his body and prompted him to leave the case in the backseat.

Collin took a quick glance at his other guest. She was passed out and in the fetal position. *Shit, no more fun for her tonight. But I can't let her freeze here.* He threw his suit coat over her, the mixture of cocaine and Champagne having taken full affect. *Well, I still have one.*

He led the other girl through the parking garage. The automatic doors slid open, and soon, they were in a maze of hallways. The two stumbled along, in search for his condominium. After wandering aimlessly through the passages and nearly being beaten by another unit resident for decorating the man's welcome mat with a cocaine/Tequila mix, Collin finally found his door.

Azure pressed against him. "Me happy you like company." She ran her hands along his chest. "Really happy...Glover-man."

Collin leaned in, giving her a deep kiss on the neck. "Let's get in...and we'll continue with this."

He opened the door, leaving his keys in the lock. The immediate darkness caught him by surprise. *Thought I left something on.* He reached to the right and flipped on the light panel. The room was still dark and *too* quiet. *Shit, what the hell is going on?* He pushed the button a second time. Again, nothing happened. Collin could feel Azure tighten her grip on his shoulder as they moved further inside the house. *No worries. Probably just burnt out.*

He turned to Azure, touching her on the arm. "Wait here."

She bit her lip and nodded. "I wait."

Collin reached out in search of the familiar leather chair he knew was just a few feet away. Collin almost fell but quickly regained his balance. *Strange...it should be right here.* He again grasped out, but a sudden shove from behind sent him catapulting through the air. His head bounced against the linoleum surface of the kitchen floor, a heavy flow of crimson erupted from his forehead.

"Uh!" He winced.

"Glover-man...you okay?" Azure inched along the wall, trying to reach him.

Collin tried to scramble to his feet, but the alcohol, combined with hitting his head, made it near impossible. "Azure, I'm over here...follow my voice."

Before he could utter another word, the glimmer of Brandon Thornley's blade flashed in front of him. The first slice severed the attorney's vocal chords. Blood sprayed in all directions, creating abstract art throughout the darkness. The second movement of the blade thrust deep into his flesh, piercing his life source. Collin Glover's spent his final seconds gasping for the precious air he would never inhale.

The scared voice of Azure Sutaki penetrated the killer's ears. Brandon Thornley rolled off his victim and focused on the dim outline of the Asian whore. *Didn't plan on this.* He sheathed the knife as he groped inside his jacket for the stun-gun. Brandon crept away from her voice, but the woman must have possessed extraordinary hearing because she suddenly stopped her movement. Brandon's pulse increased, and his heart started to race. *Let her go...too dark to tell who I am.*

The woman, satisfied the noise was from Collin Glover, again started to walk in the downed man's direction. "Glover-man, you play games with Azure? Me no like so much." Azure fumbled through her coat, pulling out a cell phone. She flipped it open and used the screen display to brighten her path.

Brandon noticed the thin beam of light and tried to stand still. Azure was only a few steps away from Collin. She raised her voice. "Glover-man, why you play trick on me, huh? Get up." She moved forward, almost on top of the dead man's body. "Hey, you no wanna play...fine. I leave then."

Curiosity got the best of her, and she bent down closer, pushing the phone towards his face. A loud shriek erupted from her. Her phone dropped to the floor. She clawed in the darkness in search of it, but panic soon overtook her. Azure tried to get to her feet. The blood pooled around Collin's body had created a slick surface, making her attempts almost futile. She screamed, managing to stand up, but her success would be short-lived.

Brandon cut her off, a few feet from the doorway. He gripped the stun-gun, sending ripples of electricity through her core. She scratched at him and was able to rip off his mask. Brandon grabbed at his face, retreating a few steps. He groped at the ground to retrieve *his* evidence. This action gave Azure a chance to break from his grasp. Even though she was more than impaired from the attack, she stumbled to the doorway. Snatching the keys that hung from the lock and hugging the wall, she attempted to flee the unknown killer.

Shit! Can't let her get away. Brandon stuffed the mask into his coat. He rushed to the door and peeked out. Azure hadn't gotten that far, and the voltage from the weapon had turned her into a sobbing mess. Brandon reached behind the door, releasing the locking device. Easing the door shut, he slipped out of the complex. He located the parking garage stairwell and knew *right* where the Asian girl was headed.

* * *

Azure was weak and kept looking back over her shoulder for the man chasing her. "Mikki, help me." Azure's voice was hoarse, and unless *someone* was within earshot, it wouldn't be noticed. "Help me...please, help me..."

She stopped to get her breath, but the pain in her side started to overwhelm her. Stripping off her coat, she tried to rid herself of anything that would slow her down. *No die here...no die here.* Azure put the house keys of Collin Glover in her right hand and let a few jut out between her fingers as she made a closed fist. The homemade weapon would be able to inflict some damage on the man, *if* she could keep up her strength.

Azure remembered where Collin had parked his car, as a thin lipped smile crossed her face. *I make it. I no want to die.* She could see the snow-covered Jaguar through the outline of the small, oval-shaped parking garage windows. *Few more step, and I safe.* She turned one more time, expecting to see the man, but the hallway was empty, and the steady sound of the heating unit was all she could hear.

Azure pushed against the double door and was exhausted of all her energy when it finally opened. She crumpled to the ground, excited the car was right in front of her. Collecting every ounce of strength she had, she shakily got to her feet. Her friend Mikki, and more importantly a cell phone, was just a step away. Azure had watched Glover use it earlier, and *she* would use it now to get help.

Staggering to the driver's side door, she pounded at the window, trying to wake Mikki from her drugged slumber. She loosened the death grip on the keys. Azure pounded even harder, but her effort was not being heard. Her hands were shaking, making it almost impossible to find the right key. Luck may have been on her side because her hands became steadier. She finally was able to find the right key. Azure turned ever so slightly to see if her attacker was anywhere close. *I safe...have to get Mikki up.* The sound of the lock clicking finally gave her a sense of security.

Azure pulled at the door, but before she could step foot inside, pain exploded in the back of her head, forcing her to the ground. She tried to stand, but *someone* had a hold of her hair and was pulling her towards the rear of the vehicle.

"Mikki, help...please," she cried.

Azure reached back to use what was left of her strength to fight off the attacker, but another searing sensation overtook her. This time, she felt the warm liquid cascade down the side of her face, watching as it flowed endlessly down the front of her shirt. All of a sudden, she stopped being dragged and began to feel like she was floating. *Am I dead?*

A moment of recognition informed her *that* wasn't the case. Her assailant was lifting her into the air and was carrying her towards the edge of the parking garage wall. She made one more feeble attempt to break away, but another wave of fire slammed into her chest. This time, she submitted to her destiny. Azure Sutaki's body plummeted onto the icy pavement of Chester Street, scraping flesh from bone. For *her,* the suffering was finally over...

CHAPTER SEVENTEEN

The Mercedes dealership was almost desolate, except for a few eager pre-holiday shoppers who didn't so much care for the car itself as they did for the status of being able to buy one. Patrick Morgan skimmed through his notes as he waited in the main reception area for the manger of the establishment. Aiden Jacobs had described a late-model Mercedes parked in front of the church, *not* the tan Caprice, which had been a consistent lead up to this point. The killer *could* be the owner of both vehicles, but his instincts told him these were *two* different men.

Graneth Kensington was the district manager of Hager Imports. He had a medium build, coupled with a blotchy complexion. The dark hair and chemically whitened teeth gave him the look of someone who *thought* he had power. He cleared his throat. "I'm ready for you now, Detective."

Patrick took a long sip of the complimentary hot chocolate before he got to his feet. *Oh, we're in a hurry now?* He left the plastic cup on the table. "Thanks, Mr. Kensington. I know *you're* a busy man, so I won't take long."

They walked along a line of mirrored glass until they stopped in front of a single doorway. This opened into a cramped hallway that led to several interior offices. Graneth Kensington waved to a few employees as he led his guest to a most spacious office. The thick, white letters engraved on the door identified him as the manager.

Graneth removed a pen from inside his pocket and waved it in front of the locking mechanism. Patrick heard a metallic sound, and within a few seconds, the door opened. He shook his head in disbelief. *Automated sensor? Just a little expensive.*

When Graneth stepped through the entryway, the overhead bank of lights automatically illuminated. The halogen lights adjusted themselves to a friendlier glow. This revealed a wall of framed portraits, the largest being a personal replica of Graneth Kensington himself. *Just a little narcissistic.* Patrick raised an eyebrow at his host.

Graneth mocked his stare but afforded an explanation anyway. "My wife had it done years ago."

Okay, so she enables him. Patrick flashed him an insincere smile. "Looks nice."

He motioned Patrick in the direction of three leather chairs. The manager pulled up a chair behind a modest computer workstation. He typed on the keypad for a few minutes before looking up. "So, Detective, I received the voice mail you left. Do you know what color and type of Mercedes you're looking for?"

Patrick thumbed through his notes. "The information says it's one of the newer models out there. Our witness thinks it's blue or dark green."

Graneth eyed his visitor with interest. "But *you're* not sure, eh?"

This guy is an asshole. Patrick shifted forward. "That's why I came to you...figured you're the only import dealer in town."

"You would be correct...I am."

Patrick flipped to a page in his notebook. "He mentioned *this* model was in the new issue of auto magazine."

A conceited smile stretched across Graneth's face. "Ah, I know which one...*this* dealership only carries two colors in that design. One is blue...the other is red."

Patrick nodded. "Many of them sold lately?"

The smile on Graneth's face faded. "Very few, Detective, very few." He pecked at the keyboard. "We sold two last month...prior to those, only one has been sold." He pointed to the computer screen.

Something at least. "Can you tell me if the sales were local?"

"We don't usually give any information on our esteemed clients. They wouldn't consider us very trustworthy if we did that, would they?"

Patrick loosened his tie. "*This* isn't a usual circumstance. It's possible evidence in an ongoing investigation—"

Graneth held a hand up. "I guess that's why they put the 'I' in investigation, my good man."

Is he fucking serious. Patrick scowled. "*You* can't help us with three names?"

Graneth stared at him. "You only need *one*."

Patrick's face was feeling hot. "Mr. Kensington, what the hell does that mean?"

"Two of the other purchases were made out of state. We have *very* loyal customers."

"And the third?"

Graneth's eyes lit up. "One of our best customers. You and he hang out in the same professional circles."

Patrick stood up. "Would you care to enlighten me?"

"I told you...our clients like that we our trustworthy—"

"You know, I can always subpoena the records if I have to."

A heavy laugh erupted from the manager. "No need for all that police drama. I'll give it to you...the client is very well-known, so not such a big deal anyway."

A colossal asshole. "Who is it, Mr. Kensington?" Patrick gritted a smile.

"The secret squirrel himself...Brandon Thornley." He leaned back in his chair. "You don't look surprised?"

Makes sense. The church was on the property Thornley owned. "I'm not...thanks for your help. Next time, don't be such an asshole about it."

Patrick stuffed his tie inside his coat pocket and hurried out the door before Graneth could say anything in return. Patrick pulled out his cell phone, as he walked towards his car.

"Morgan, what did you find out?" Commander Cromartie's voice sounded hoarse.

"Dealership has three purchases for this type of Mercedes. Two of them not local, but the third belongs to Brandon Thornley."

"He owns the old church property, *correct?*" Cromartie's voiced raised an octave.

Shit. He's gonna shut me down before I even get started. "Yes, but I still think it needs to be looked at."

"Talk to him, but tread lightly. We don't have anything but *his* car at the scene...and it is *his* property. You got it, Morgan?"

"Gotcha."

"Good, we'll look like major fuck-ups if we start accusing this guy without solid evidence."

"Understood, boss."

"I'm serious, Morgan...don't screw this up." The line clicked dead.

Brandon Thornley was a key-to-the-city type of guy, and Patrick was ninety-nine percent certain there was a legitimate reason he was at spotted at the scene. Then again, there was always that one percent...

CHAPTER EIGHTEEN

Donovan Petrie parked his Caprice along the side street in front of his next victim's home. The neighbors wouldn't take a second glance at him; they would assume by the make and model, he was investigating *someone* for *something*. The last of the sunlight had disappeared, leaving bitter cold and darkness in its place. Donovan stared at the house. Only a faint glow from the upstairs bedroom gave any evidence of life.

He reached over and plucked up the folder on the passenger seat. Lucky for him, his security access had already been established, making it almost *too* easy to research the biker wannabe. After all, that's what Marty Brocklin was. The former semi-pro wrestler and convicted cocaine dealer now was playing the role of an angry biker who enjoyed abusing women. *He really needs to be put out of his misery*. Marty Brocklin had such a tarnished past, the world would hardly mourn *his* loss.

Donovan knew the man was alone. The girlfriend had been carrying an overnight bag when she left a few hours earlier. *Not coming back tonight*, he thought. Donovan turned off the engine and slipped out into the cold. He adjusted his backpack as he crept to the rear of the house and smiled as he eyed the door handle and its absence of a secondary lock system. *Just pathetic*. The killer removed a few tools from inside his jacket, making quick work of the cheap lock. As he entered, the strong odor of stale beer and burnt popcorn attacked him. Even in darkness, Donovan could tell the ritual of good housekeeping was not a priority for the couple.

He slipped off the backpack and placed it next to the stairwell. The house was almost too quiet, but after looking around on the main floor, Donovan knew the felon was more than likely upstairs, probably taking part in medicating himself with *some* type of recreational drugs. He picked up the backpack, unzipping a medium-sized compartment. The newly purchased blade glistened. He ran his hand along the steel edge, being careful to avoid any bloodletting. Donovan sheathed the knife and strapped it to his right ankle. He opened another pocket on the bag, removing the ceremonial candles, plastic sheeting and rolled barbwire. Donovan was about to create a distraction to lure Marty downstairs, when he felt a vibration in his coat pocket. *Interesting timing.* He withdrew the phone and stared at the blue screen. *One new message.*

Donovan clicked the tracking ball. He licked his lips in anticipation.

Donovan, sorry to bother at this late hour. Just wanted to say thank you for taking the job with us.

He started to laugh but quickly stifled it. Donovan typed a few lines and hit the send key. A few minutes later, Brandon Thornley sent a follow-up message.

What am I doing awake? Going over all of these friend requests I haven't checked in a while. Yes to the drink after work tomorrow. Thanks for asking.

Donovan smiled. After typing in a few more words, he stuck the phone back into his jacket. *Hmm, we already are becoming friends.* He took a few deep breaths, and his focus on the task at hand, soon was back into the forefront. The killer made little noise as he unrolled the plastic sheeting and spread it across the dirty kitchen tile. When the set-up was completed, he slipped off his boots and placed them adjacent to the back door. *No bloody footprints to track.* Returning to the backpack, he removed a pair of dual-strength leather gloves. *Don't need any of my blood left here.*

Donovan moved through the residence with smooth and calculated timing. He stopped at the bottom of the stairwell. *Fuck...you gotta be kidding.* The steps were constructed of bare wood, and any attempt to ascend them would alert his victim to his presence. Donovan retraced his steps. He glanced at the large television on the opposite of the room. *What a wonderful idea.* He leaped back, as somewhere in the room a high pitched ringing started to sound. *Damn phone's gonna spoil my plan.* Donovan heard several shouts of profanity as the pounding of the floorboards told him his prey was now awake.

Marty Brocklin's half-naked, tattooed figure appeared at the foot of the stairs. "Who the fuck is calling at this hour?" he yelled to no one in particular.

Donovan could hear personal belongings being thrown chaotically as the man searched in disgust for the handset. "Bastard, there you are." The ringing ceased, indicating Marty had found what he was looking for. "Hello."

Donovan couldn't hear the person on the other end, but whatever they said upset him even more.

"How in shit's sake did you get arrested? Are you that fucking stupid? Don't fucking answer that...I'll be down to bail your ass out." Marty slammed down the phone.

Donovan could hear the man rumble in his direction. He quietly unsheathed the weapon, watching as the man came closer.

Marty Brocklin stepped through the kitchen entryway. He flipped on the light switch and reeled back in surprise. "What in the hell—"

Donovan snuck in from behind, and before Marty "wannabe biker" Brocklin could defend himself, the barbwire had encircled his throat. Not even muffled screams escaped the man as Donovan tightened his grip even further. The razors cut through the man's skin, leaving a crimson river in its path. Donovan forced his prey to the ground with one hand and with his other thrust the blade into his chest. Donovan didn't stop putting pressure on the knife until the hilt was the only thing showing.

He swung around, straddling Marty Brocklin. A few minutes ago, the man had his anger on display. *Now* a look of fear had taken its place. *Just like all my other victims*, Donovan thought, peering into his eyes, relishing the moment that Marty Brocklin's life source drained away. *Ready or not, Brandon Thornley...soon, you will be mine.*

CHAPTER NINETEEN

Patrick Morgan had contacted Brandon Thornley's office earlier. The Security Director had been more than happy to accommodate him by answering his questions. *Doesn't sound like he has anything to hide.*

Patrick took a glimpse of his watch. *Just a little early.* The two security officers stationed at the front entrance looked more like professional football players than the cliché most people had of the occupation. The Italian suits were, no doubt, a lot more expensive than anything Patrick would *ever* own. He displayed his credentials, as one of the officers put a hand out to stop his progress.

"Sir, your escort will be here momentarily."

Ouch. Nobody trusts the police anymore. Patrick smiled. "No problem, I'll just take a seat over there...if that's okay?" He pointed to the lobby vending area.

The officer nodded and ignored Patrick from that point. Patrick grabbed a cup of coffee from the machine. He found a seat and scanned his notes. He was halfway through when loud chimes started to play in the pocket of his blazer. *Oh shit...I knew I forgot something.* "Yes, sir."

Commander Cromartie's voice filled the small handset. "Morgan, I'm on a three way call with Sergeant Holly Weinens. A woman's body was found a few hours ago...right in the middle of Chester Street."

Patrick closed the notebook. "A homicide?"

Cromartie cleared his throat. "The initial indication was suicide...but there were some other wounds that were not from the apparent fall."

Patrick scratched his head. "What kind?"

Holly Weinens' rich southern accent came on the line. "Detective, the girl had some deep lacerations. One was just above her lower back, and the other was on her right rib cage."

"Morgan, the knife wounds look similar to the *other* cases we're working on...that's why I called you on this."

"Any weapons found at the scene?" Patrick asked.

"None, so far..." Sergeant Weinens intervened, her voice drifting off.

"So, this girl is *possibly* bleeding to death and propels herself from some roof?"

"Parking garage, sir...attached to apartment complex," Weinens corrected him.

"Morgan, looks like someone *threw* her off. I have the County Medical Examiner doing the autopsy now. Depending on what she finds...may want you to be there, too."

Still chasing this lead. Patrick rolled his eyes. He ignored his supervisor as he posed a question to the female supervisor.

"Sergeant Weinens, what time was she discovered?"

"My patrol corporal said just after six o'clock this morning."

Obvious commuting hours. "What do we know about the girl?"

Commander Cromartie was back on point. "Her name is Azure Sutaki. She worked at the local casino as an entertainment consultant."

Simple translation...a high-price call girl. "Sir, maybe get with the manager over there and check out if her services were needed by outside sources."

"Agreed. I'll send some people to get witness statements. If I hear anything from the M.E.'s office, I'll give you a ring."

"Great, boss. Sergeant Weinens, keep me posted if you come across any more information on the dead girl."

"Sure thing, Detective."

Cromartie thanked the patrol supervisor, ending her portion of the call. "Morgan, you see Brandon Thornley yet?"

"I'm waiting here now. The good director even set me up with an escort."

Cromartie laughed. "You some kind of important person?"

"It would appear so."

"Well, like I said *before*—"

"I know, boss…kid gloves."

"Morgan, I got a call on the desk line. I'll check in with you later."

Thanks for warning me. "10-4, sir."

Patrick flipped the phone closed. He waited for several more minutes before Monty York whistled in his direction. "I see *they* sent the super-duper sleuth on this one." Monty grinned.

He had known Monty since Patrick was naïve rookie, and the elder officer had taken an interest with his interrogation techniques. Patrick was saddened when the man left the department for greener pastures. The man was straight forward about *everything*.

"How the hell are you, old man?" Patrick grasped the man's hand in a fierce handshake.

"Can't complain, son."

"How is the gig with Thornley?" Patrick smiled.

The burly man ran a hand over his shaved head. "Pat, this organization has some good people. Brandon Thornley treats us like family."

All families all have secrets. Patrick folded his arms. "Monty, is the guy a straight shooter?" *He won't lie to me.*

"Always has been with me. The man *is* a little odd, but who the hell isn't now-a-days?" Monty grinned.

True. Patrick glanced at his watch. "Well, lead the way. I just have a few questions for him…nothing too major."

Monty winked. "It's *not* like he killed anyone, right?"

Not that you know of. "Nothing like that."

"Onward then, youngster," Monty jested, leading him through the hallway and to the office of Langston Security Solution's Security Director.

* * *

Brandon Thornley's nerves were on edge. Between cutting himself while shaving and spilling his morning latte on his new shirt, the day so far had been one to forget. The call from Detective Patrick Morgan could have been the determining factor for a majority of the extra stress. Brandon had spent a good part of the morning going over the reasons why the man would need to speak with him. *The bodies are buried deep enough. That can't be it.* He had been very careful to avoid detection when he was anywhere near the church. Maybe all of his preparation for each sacred kill was flawed. *Maybe someone did see me.*

Brandon reached into his desk and picked up the hand mirror. The makeup had done substantial in masking the scratches, but they were *still* going to be visible, *especially* for a seasoned investigator. Good thing he had a second change of clothes at the office, and more importantly, his wife didn't question his explanation about not coming home last night.

He lifted up the mirror and grimaced. *Time for another touch up. I really should have let the bitch go.* Brandon knew from experience that his DNA *would* be found underneath the woman's fingernails, but he also knew *his* blood work hadn't been taken for several years, and this gave him a slight hope he would stay undiscovered.

Brandon opened a side drawer and removed the bottle of flesh-colored makeup. He dabbed at the right side of his face until the colors meshed and the marks were almost unnoticeable. He raised his head in time to see the blurred frame of Monty York and what he presumed to be Detective Patrick Morgan at the entrance to his office. Brandon shoved the mirror and makeup into the drawer and slammed it shut. He straightened out his suit coat, buttoning it up to hide the stained shirt.

A forceful knock came from the front door. "Sir, your appointment is here."

Brandon's hands were shaking. *Get a grip, or this could be it.* He took a few deep breaths. "Monty, come in."

Monty was accompanied by the slender but well built Patrick Morgan. The man was wearing an inexpensive blue blazer and a pair of dark pants in the same price range as the blazer. *Not exactly a power suit for investigations.*

Brandon stood and offered an outstretched hand in the man's direction. "Pleased to make your acquaintance, Detective. Monty, would you excuse us?"

"Yes, boss. If you need me, I'll be at the security desk."

Patrick waited for his long-time friend to exit before he addressed the security mogul. He smiled in almost an apologetic fashion. "Thank you for taking time out of your busy day. I promise *this* won't take long."

Brandon flashed a smile. "You know, when I was in law enforcement, and *I* used the word promise in regards to someone's time, it was *always* longer and *more* tedious than both of us expected."

"This is pretty simple and straight forward stuff. Just need to clarify some things." Patrick smiled, removing his notebook.

Nothing is ever simple and straight forward. "Ask away."

"Sir, I'm investigating the murder of Jamie Brooks. The body was found on the third floor of United Ministries. I think the property belongs to you now?"

It does. Brandon nodded. "Yes, my father left it to me after he passed."

Patrick jotted down some notes. "Do *you* know Jamie Brooks?"

"Can't say the name is familiar to me." *Very interesting.*

"How much time do you spend time on the property, sir?" Patrick looked up from his notes.

Brandon leaned back. *More than you could imagine.* "Detective, I drive by there a few times a week. The place is a nightmare...and I've been talking to a contractor about demolition."

"So, would you say there's a significant amount time spent there?" The officer cocked his head.

Brandon tapped his fingers on the desk. "Just enough to make sure the graveyard isn't being vandalized by the local misfits." *Somebody saw the car.*

"Graveyard?" Patrick asked.

He can't think I'm that stupid. "Yes, my father is buried there. Like *I* said, I would prefer not to have it vandalized by undesirables."

The serious look on Patrick's face started to fade. "We do have a few of those. Sir, there was a witness who saw your Mercedes on the property the night Jamie Brook's body was discovered."

Brandon stopped the tapping. "So, naturally, I'm the first one *you* need to speak with."

Patrick leaned forward in the chair. "Naturally."

Brandon smiled. "Well, ask away, Mr. Morgan."

Patrick turned to a blank page in his notebook. "Mr. Thornley, have you seen anyone on your property that shouldn't be there?"

Brandon shook his head. "Not that I recall. I'm usually the *only* person who's brave enough to wander through that mess."

Patrick scribbled on the pad. "I know it's your property and everything, but can you tell me what you were doing there the other night at that late of hour?"

Burying a body. "Of course. Every Christmas, Dad and I had a tradition to put holiday wreaths at the headstone of each person in the graveyard. I still do that...and the night in question was when *I* was carrying on his legacy."

Patrick looked up. "That's admirable."

Brandon folded his arms. "Tell me, Detective...don't you have family traditions?"

Patrick fidgeted in his chair. "Me? I'm not a big Christmas guy and all...my daughter and wife love it, though...so I go along for *them*."

Very interesting. "Sorry, I didn't mean to pry," Brandon said.

Patrick flipped the notebook closed. "Sir, I think you have given me everything *I* need. It all makes sense to me. I told you this would be quick." He reached across the table, waiting for a return handshake.

Fucking hands are still shaking. Brandon reached at his belt for his cell phone. "I have to take this, Detective, if you would excuse me."

Patrick withdrew his hand. "No problem. I'll let myself out. Thanks for your time. If I have any more questions…I'll be in touch."

How did he know the Mercedes was mine? Brandon smiled. "Anything you need…just let me know." He returned to his pretend phone call.

The detective waved as he left the office. "Thanks, I will."

Brandon waited for the door to close before he threw the cell phone on the desk. *Fucker left in a hurry. I wonder why?* He hadn't noticed the small beads of sweat dripping down his neck, until he realized the water droplets were landing on the collar of his shirt. He wiped at them, but then was enlightened by something else. His vehicle had dealership tags, and the only person who knew it belonged to him was Graneth Kensington. The thought of the Englishman providing information about him to the local authorities wasn't sitting well with him at all.

CHAPTER TWENTY

Patrick Morgan had been summoned by Commander Cromartie to meet him at the Harris County Memorial Hospital. Patrick still had the meeting with Brandon Thornley on his mind and thought it was strange how it appeared the man had been wearing makeup. *Rich people are odd.* Patrick passed through the gates of HCMH, recalling the local paper printing a recent story on the facility. The medical care was touted to be the finest in the Midwest, and the influx of out-of-state patients was an indicator of that fact. The multiple structures were designed with futuristic overtones, and many people thought the facility looked like something out of a science fiction movie.

Patrick had only been here a few times, but his eyes were always fixated to the man-made lake surrounding the property. In the summer months, the lake's water was so clear, people would just sit at the bank, watching the fish swim like there was no tomorrow. Patrick focused his attention to the slate-colored building behind the main hospital. This was a separate structure built *especially* for the morgue and its examination laboratory.

According to Commander Cromartie, the local medical examiner had completed the autopsy on Azure Sutaki, and the findings were *quite* revealing. He pulled the unmarked in a spot designated for emergency vehicles. Patrick noticed his supervisor was already parked. He was standing a few feet from the loading dock and was engaged in conversation with an attractive, slender blonde. She appeared to be in her late thirties, and even though the temperatures were near freezing, she was dressed in just a white turtleneck and black pants. *Braver than me.* Patrick stepped out to meet the two.

Cromartie nodded as he approached. "Morgan, this is Dr. Abbey Krieger. She's the medical examiner assigned to Azure Sutaki and Jamie Brooks."

Dr. Krieger smiled at Patrick as she rubbed her hands together. "Okay, gentlemen, let's step inside. Your latest victim has a very interesting story to tell us."

Patrick and Cromartie followed her through the dock door and down into a service elevator. The strong scent of pine oil filled the spacious conveyance. They stepped out into a waiting room, which was furnished with a large leather couch and matching chairs; a computer workstation; and, to top it off, a full-size kitchen. *Better than my first apartment.* Patrick was unaware he had made a face, but Dr. Krieger noticed and smiled.

She explained. "Detective, this is designed to ease the families in their time of grief. Unlike most hospitals, and the unfriendly surroundings of a cold and lifeless room, *we* have found this to be more soothing."

Hmm. Death and soothing in the same sentence. "All you need is a big screen T.V."

"Touché, Detective, touché." Dr. Krieger chuckled.

Cromartie wasn't as amused. He glared in his direction but kept his comments to himself.

Dr. Krieger led them through a long corridor, stopping at two sets of double doors. She removed a magnetic card from her front pocket and swiped it through a card reader just to the right of the entrance.

Pretty high tech for the dead. Patrick glanced up, looking for a surveillance camera. The locking system disengaged, and soon, the three were inside. Patrick made a whistling sound. *Definitely sci-fi attributes here.* The room was encased in a silver sheen. Even the floor appeared to be covered with it.

A medium-sized computer work station was in one corner of the room. On the wall directly above it hung three framed documents; one Patrick made out with genuine interest. *University of Iowa...very prestigious.* Patrick gawked at the accompaniment of tools of her trade that hung from various hooks. One in particular really caught his attention.

Dr. Krieger noticed him staring, as she enlightened him. "Bone saw, Detective…you ever see one before?"

"No." Patrick re-focused his attention to the large picture-window-sized mirror directly across from the entrance.

Dr. Krieger handed them each a white gown. Before he had an opportunity to ask about it, she interjected. "Detectives, stainless steel makes the area easy to sterilize."

Cromartie voiced what Patrick had been thinking. "Why is that necessary?"

Dr. Krieger raised a brow. "With the current flu, and *its* killing potential, *this* room limits the spread of the disease."

Good enough answer as any. Patrick slipped on the gown, then pointed to the mirror. "Why a two-way mirror?"

Dr. Krieger tied her gown. "Sometimes, we have students assist with examinations. The mirror is used by their fellow physicians to watch them and review their skills."

Patrick nodded. "A whole *new* meaning to Big Brother is watching."

"Just for learning, Detective. Nothing *so* ominous as that." Dr. Krieger walked over and pushed a button on the wall. A door slid open, leading to the examination room. "This way."

Patrick and Cromartie stepped through the opening. The door closed behind them.

This interior was similar to the room they had just left, except along with the two medical carts and matching silver slabs. The far wall housed fifty refrigeration units. The cubicles, reserved for the dead, were stacked five high and ten across. Patrick had *never* seen this many units before and figured *all* of New Haven's deceased probably came here.

Dr. Krieger cleared her throat. "Detective Morgan, like I was explaining to the Commander here…I was assigned the Jamie Brooks case, and *now*, our latest victim, Azure Sutaki." She walked over and pulled open one of the refrigeration units.

Patrick felt a sudden change in the room temperature. This caused cold chills to fill his body.

The medical examiner grinned. "The units are kept at a lower temp, so when opened, they lower the core of the room."

Patrick shivered. "Great to know, Doc."

"Just give me a few minutes, and I'll have Ms. Sutaki on the table."

Dr. Krieger pulled a cart from the unit all the way out. She removed a remote from her pocket and pushed one of the buttons. A loud grinding sound came from one of the ceiling panels, and within thirty seconds, an opening had replaced the tile. She pushed another button, and a large mechanical crane lowered to the center of the room. There were several metal clips extending from it. Dr. Krieger reached out and grabbed one of the clips. She pulled on it, as the clip loosened from the device. An elongated black covered wire exposed itself as the medical examiner yanked on it, making it long enough to reach one of the rings on the metal cart. She repeated the process two more times, until all the wires were attached to the corresponding rings. When the task was completed, she pressed another button on the remote. The motor hummed as the cart was lifted into the air and hovered above the metal slate table. Dr. Krieger guided the cart with her hand, until she was satisfied it would center with perfection. One more push of a button lowered the cold slab onto the table. She undid the hooks and pushed the crane away from the table.

"Gather round. I *hope* you guys don't have weak stomachs," she said.

Patrick took one side of the table as Cromartie went to the other. Dr. Krieger removed the thin white covering from the upper body of Azure Sutaki's corpse. Most of the flesh on the woman's face had been scraped off, and only fragments of her once-perfect teeth still remained in place. Her neck was grossly off centered, and a bone had pierced through, just below her throat. *Note to self: never jump from a building,* Patrick thought.

Cromartie flinched and let out a cough.

The medical examiner noticed his reaction. "Commander, you okay to continue?"

"Yes, go ahead, Doctor."

She pointed to the woman's neck. "Gentlemen, the fall produced several broken bones; only *this* one here would have been fatal upon impact."

Patrick scratched at his head. "Just *that* one?"

Dr. Krieger lowered the rest of the sheet, as the familiar "Y" incision was more noticeable. "Yes, Detective. Most people jump feet first off a building...this girl, as you can see, landed face-first."

"Ouch." Patrick wrinkled his face.

"Ouch is right." She touched several deep lacerations on the woman's scalp and lower right side. "Detective Morgan, these were caused by a very sharp object in excess of four inches." The medical examiner peeled back the flesh, exposing the protruding organs. "Come closer...you see the wound and where the organ was struck—"

"Her lung." Patrick exhaled.

She nodded. "This wound would slow her down...considerably."

Dr. Krieger rolled Azure Sutaki onto her side. "You see this? An exact duplicate wound...*this* time piercing the kidney."

"Which of them happened first?"

She pointed to a gash on Azure's head. "This one did...the girl tried to run but was already bleeding significantly, then the killer struck her again, this time in the lung...ending any further resistance."

Patrick stared at his supervisor. "She never had a chance."

Dr. Krieger looked up. "But we do have *one* thing the killer left behind."

Cromartie smiled. "The bastard left some blood at the scene?"

The medical examiner held up the right hand of Azure Sutaki. "Take a look here...underneath her fingernails."

Both investigators leaned closer.

"Is that what I think it is?"

"I'm running some DNA tests on a small sample I took earlier, Detective Morgan. She was out there a while, and in *really* damp conditions. I'm hopeful, after we get the results back, we'll enough to get a match." Dr. Krieger looked down into the abyss that once was the face of a woman filled with life.

The three finished discussion on how Azure Sutaki spent her final moments, as Patrick Morgan kept thinking, W*hy was she on the roof that time of night, and more importantly, who was with her?*

CHAPTER TWENTY-ONE

Donovan Petrie adjusted the red and blue tie. He looked up from his monitor and scanned the room, eyeing several of the other employees. They appeared to be drawn to their workstations, like worker honeybees gathering nectar for their Queen. *This* hive, however, was governed by a King. *A soon to be dead king.*

Brandon Thornley had given *him* a leadership position and authority over this motley collection of security consultants. He had praised Donovan's talents to the company board. It had been a unanimous decision to place Donovan in charge of assessing viable threats Langston Security Solutions would encounter, both here and abroad. This would be the perfect cover for him, especially when the local authorities found Brandon tied up in ritualistic fashion, like all of his other conquests. *Almost too perfect of a plan.*

Donovan had the distinct feeling *he* was being watched, and *this* disturbed him. He turned ever so slightly, locating his new admirer. The majority of *most* men would consider her to be a rather homely woman. The tousled red hair, thick brown-rimmed glasses, and her poor fashion sense would, without a doubt, put her *first* in line for a makeover with all of the women's leading magazines. But for Donovan, *he* saw something unique and alluring. He made eye contact with her, but she quickly looked away. The only other female who *he* remembered staring at him like this was Tamara, the petite bookseller. *That was a true waste.*

He turned back to his computer screen and brought up the *administrative option menu*. Donovan typed in his password. A list of administration privileges appeared, then he clicked on a folder labeled *Employee Profiles.* His eyes lit up as he scrolled through the various pictures of his new employees. Donovan stopped when he found the photo matching the girl across the room. He scoured the onscreen information. The woman was not only physically intriguing; she had quite an academic background, which would intimidate even the most senior leadership in the organization. *Brandon seems to hire all the best.* Alexis Loggins was *someone* Donovan wanted to get to know *very* well. A few quick clicks of the mouse, and he had a color picture of her, along with her biographical detail. Donovan stuffed the paperwork into a brown folder and shoved it his laptop bag. *Research for later.*

He finished a few more tasks Brandon had requested and was about to leave for the day when his cell phone vibrated. He glanced down at the screen. *Shit, I almost forgot about that.* Donovan logged off and collected his things. He typed a quick message in return and hurried towards the door. Donovan took one more glance at the red-haired woman as she instinctively looked up. A thin smile escaped from her. *A very intriguing woman indeed.*

* * *

Embassy Bistro was where the men and women of Langston Security Solutions would congregate for their after work gossip and take part in a libation or two. The company had added the establishment to their private food court, in hopes of promoting "the people who work hard together should play hard together" motto. Donovan spotted Brandon sitting at a table towards the rear of the eatery. He fought through several people crowding the bar until making it to his supervisor's table.

Brandon laughed. "You never want to get between our employees and alcohol. A combination good does not make."

Alcohol is a weakness of mine. Donovan slipped off his jacket. "Thanks for the tip. I'll *have* to bring my stun gun with me next time." *Why's he got makeup on his face? Definitely egotistical.*

Brandon flashed a devilish grin. "Ah, my favorite toy, as well."

That was a weird statement. "Thanks for inviting me." Donovan raised his hand to get the waitress's attention. He ordered a Blue Hawaiian for himself and a Long Island Ice Tea for Brandon.

Brandon chuckled. "Nice choice. You want me to call her back and make sure she doesn't forget the umbrella?"

"Ouch, boss."

Brandon tapped him on the arm. "Just screwing with you...and another thing, while we are *here*, call me Brandon. I consider this place informal."

I'd rather call you "dead man." Donovan nodded. "I'm all for informal."

The dark-haired waitress returned with the drinks. Brandon slipped her a few bills.

He raised his glass. "Well, let's make a toast...to new beginnings."

More like tragic endings. Donovan raised his glass in return. "New beginnings, it is."

The two indulged in several conversations, ranging from family to retirement. Two hours and three Blue Hawaiians later, Donovan was actually enjoying the man's company. He started to rise up from his chair when a picture of the deceased Marty Brocklin flashed on the LCD screen above the bar. Donovan leaned closer and heard the following.

New Haven Police uncovered a grisly scene earlier this evening when they were summoned to the residence at 617 Evergreen. Police say at 5:30 p.m., the woman living at this address identified as Lacey Steen came home and discovered the body of her boyfriend, one Marty Brocklin. He was thirty-nine years old and a long-time resident of New Haven. EyeSpot 5 News has heard from an unidentified source the crime scene appeared to look like something out of a modern-day horror film. New Haven Police Detectives continue to investigate at this hour, still searching for leads in this frightening discovery. I asked around the neighborhood, and a majority of the residents described Marty Brocklin as a quiet man who kept to himself. Again, to repeat the breaking news, Marty Brocklin, age thirty-nine, found dead tonight on the city's lower East side. Stay tuned for further developments. This is Rich Wolf for EyeSpot 5 News.

Donovan watched as the screen went back to scheduled programming. *Doesn't appear anyone saw me.* He slipped on his jacket.

Brandon stood up. "Wow. You know, I spent several years in law enforcement, and the world just gets *crazier* every day. Seems like we just become more animalistic as time passes."

"*Some* people are probably born that way." Donovan felt a little woozy. *Way too much rum.*

Brandon eyed his new friend with interest. "Born evil…you mean?"

I know one person who was. "Probably not. I'm a *little* drunk, so don't pay any attention to my ramblings."

Brandon smiled. "No, I think *you're* correct. Some people are destined to do good…while others are on the opposite of the spectrum."

No lecture, please. "Comic book good versus evil?"

"Donovan, don't you ever get the urge just to do bad things?"

You'll soon know. "Like running a stop light?"

Brandon put a hand around his shoulder as they walked to the front of the establishment. "Worse. I was thinking more like…hurting somebody on *purpose*."

Deep fucking thoughts from a closet sociopath. "Maybe once or twice." Donovan's face was serious.

"It's like a *hunger,* Donovan…a hunger that *can't* be satiated." Brandon Thornley's eyes lit up like a kid in a candy store.

Donovan stepped into the fresh air. "Don't let people hear you say that *too* loud…they might think you're some deranged killer." He laughed.

Brandon returned the gesture. "I would have a *perfect* cover though."

I know I'm nuts, but this guy has actually thought this out. Donovan lit a cigar. "It's time for us both to get the hell out of here. We *both* are just a little intoxicated."

"Until tomorrow then?"

Offer him a ride home and kill him. Donovan raised his cigar. *Too soon, no alibi.* "Tomorrow it is."

"Hey, you need a lift?" Brandon jingled his keys.

"Thanks, but…I don't have far to go. I should be asking if *you* need a ride."

Brandon placed his hands in front of him and pretended he was handcuffed. "Don't arrest me, Mr. Officer."

Not exactly what I was thinking. "Get out of here." Donovan waved as he started walking away from his supervisor.

It was thought provoking how Brandon had been almost full of excitement when he mentioned hurting people and having a hunger that couldn't be met. Brandon Thornley sounded like he had a dark secret hiding underneath, and Donovan was curious to find it out what it was.

CHAPTER TWENTY-TWO

Even though the local weather channel had issued a winter storm warning, and the snow was falling with reckless abandon, Ravine's Goldmine had a line extending from its front entrance, through the parking lot, and finally ending on the adjacent street. The patrons were in attendance for the casino's annual Winter Giveaway Extravaganza. The marketing and advertising experts had given it *this* name in hopes that more novice gamblers would pay more attention to the "giveaway" part and try their luck to win millions. In past years, the casino would draw people from all over the Midwest to attend, but due to the slow economy, this year's staple was mostly in-state clientele.

I'd just throw my money at the place as I drove by. Patrick Morgan was here because an unidentified caller contacted the office. They reported the late Azure Sutaki was seen playing the slots in the accompaniment of a local attorney on the night of her death. A New Haven Patrol Officer had originally responded to check on the lead, but the management of the casino had been persistent in speaking with a *detective* about a possible suspect. *Here I am. Drugs and prostitutes usually lead to bigger things.*

Patrick glared at the anxious mob as he pushed towards the security booth. Several people gave him looks of disdain. One even offered to engage him in a physical altercation. Patrick pointed to his badge. The man suddenly vanished within the sea of people. The detective stopped at the security booth and fished out his credentials. A pock-marked security officer leaned forward to get a better visual. He mumbled something into his hand-held microphone. A few seconds later, another security team member arrived and escorted him off to the side. Patrick smiled. He tried to make conversation, but the man just stood there in silence. A few minutes later, the casino owner herself was walking towards him.

What did I do to deserve this honor? Constance Ravine had the looks and body most women in their mid-forties would die for. Her silky, dark hair and slender figure suited her well. She was dressed for the holidays: her red gown highlighted her physique with perfection. A slit down each side exposed her tanned flesh. Style was *one* aspect of Constance Ravine's life that needed little improvement. Patrick's wife had shown him an article in the *New Haven Minute*, which spotlighted Constance and her rise to success. The woman was the heir to one of the largest clothing designers in the United States.

Tiomaotta, Incorporated, was known for supplying attire for famous actors and actresses. The various lines and fashions were becoming all the rage, and soon, the company would become global. Constance had been groomed from birth to take over, but after she completed her fashion degree and spent a few years in the business, she lost her desire for it. Her late-night binge drinking and vicious gambling habit at various casinos catapulted her interest in the industry. It was enough to move her away from the East and create another path for her life.

Constance used a portion of her earnings to open Ravine's, and since it's inception, the business had flourished at an alarming rate. The addition of V.I.P. suites for select guests was something Constance wanted, but her many high-dollar clients also had a strong taste for beautiful women. This put prostitution and illegal drugs into play, and of *course*, Constance had a take in *all* the proceeds.

Constance had a devastating smile; it almost made Patrick Morgan lose sight why he was there.

She offered a firm handshake. "Follow me, Detective." She looked past him and through the windows as they walked. "Look at those wonderful people tonight. Should be a gala of a time. All this money…just ready to be given away."

Don't you mean collected? Patrick followed her to the elevator, noticing the dress clinging tightly as she moved. "Well, you can't win if you don't play." Patrick chuckled.

She flipped her hair back, exposing her neckline. "How true, dear Mr. Policeman."

Constance stopped the elevator on the top floor and escorted him to a large conference room. It was set up much like most executives would have done, but the flavor was unique with the multiple video displays and a fully stocked bar. She pulled out a chair for him as she grabbed a bottle of wine and two glasses.

He raised a hand. "None for me. I stopped drinking a few years ago."

She cracked a devilish grin. "Tsk, tsk. *I* surely don't want to be responsible for *you* falling off the wagon." She tipped the bottle filling both glasses. "Just more for me, then." Constance winked.

Patrick pulled out the black and white photo of Azure Sutaki. He set it down on the table so Constance had no choice but to stare into the dead girl's eyes. "Ms. Ravine, what can *you* tell me about her?"

Constance ran her finger along the edges of the goblet. "Azure was going to school and needed a job, so I hired her as a slot attendant."

A play on words if there ever was one. "Most of your slot machine employees don't end up dead, do they?"

Constance took a long sip of the wine. "No. The girl also did some dancing for some of our prestigious clients."

Slot attendant and dancing don't really go together. "So, *you* hired her as a stripper?"

"No, *we* don't employ strippers *here,* Detective." She stood up and walked behind the bar, bending to search through a cabinet drawer.

The slit in her dress made it near impossible for Patrick to look away. Intimacy between him and Coral had been non-existent since Kelsey had gotten worse. It would be so easy to take what Constance was offering, but a picture of his girls at home flashed through his head, sending him back to reality.

Constance was trying hard, though. She bent down even further to give him a better view. "I also own the Night of Pleasure party service…if *you* didn't know." She removed a pink folder. She stood up and sauntered over. Constance slapped the file on the table. "If consenting adults want to play…I *certainly* don't intend to stop them." She adjusted her dress in a playful way. "Detective Morgan, I'm a sucker for anything resembling romance." She took another drink.

Very convenient to have another business. Patrick shook his head. "So between Ms. Sutaki's duties here and with her *other* job, which *you* also employ her…she ends up dead?"

Constance finished off the first glass. "That's why I wanted to talk to you, Detective. I got a telephone call a few nights ago. The man wanted two Asian ladies for a party he was hosting downtown. At the last minute, he decides to rent one of our suites here to conduct the festivities."

Patrick scratched his brow. "Isn't that a conflict of interest for you?"

Constance smiled. "Depends how *you* look at it. The man was willing to pay for both of *my* services, so I have no regrets on making money. However, in retrospect, if I had the option to go back in time, I wouldn't have let her do the party." She shifted in her seat.

Too late. She's dead. "Why do you say that?" Patrick poised his pen above the notebook. "Is that because your actions got her killed?"

"I'm not responsible for her death. I have…many girls who work for me. I have never had a problem—"

"Until now."

"Yes, until now. She didn't jump off that roof."

She seems to know something. "What do *you* think happened?"

Constance brought the other goblet to her lips, pausing before she drank. "The man who had the party was also a regular customer at the casino. I saw them talking several times when Azure *should* have been working."

Patrick flipped a page of the pad. "Did you witness any altercations or anything odd?"

Constance took a deep drink from the glass, then shook her head. "Nothing direct, but the guy gave me goose bumps every time I saw him."

"You got a name for me?" *Let's see how important money is to her.*

"Collin Glover. I know he works in the legal field."

Patrick had seen billboards of the man scattered throughout New Haven, so he wasn't surprised when he heard his name mentioned. "So, Mr. Glover and Azure were dating?"

Constance smirked. "I don't think so. More *like* long term fuck buddies."

Not surprising at all. "But again, no altercations in the casino, to the best of your knowledge?"

Constance tapped her fingers on the table. "None. The man just gave off a weird vibe."

Patrick nodded. "Excuse me for a minute." He stood up and unclipped his cell phone from his belt.

A few seconds later, Commander Cromartie was on the line. "Morgan, if you're calling, you found something."

"Apparently, the dead woman was seen with local sleaze ball attorney, Collin Glover. Sounds like an ongoing affair."

"Morgan, do *you* think he pitched her from the roof?"

He's the only suspect. "Not sure, but let's dispatch a few officers to his residence and find out?"

Cromartie coughed. "I'm on it. I'll text you his address, so we can meet."

"I have a few more questions for the casino owner, then I'll head your way."

"10-4. Maybe we can even link him to the other cases."

"Wouldn't that be perfect?"

Cromartie let out a nervous laugh. "Not likely, huh?"

"I wouldn't bet my career on it." Patrick flipped the phone off.

He returned to his host. Constance took a look at him, then finished the remaining wine.

"You think what I do is wrong. I've seen *that* look before. Just like my dad, when I told him I was quitting the company."

Patrick stared at her. "I'm here to find out who did this to Azure Sutaki. I think it's safe to say we *both* know what really goes on here."

Constance bit her lip. "Proving it *is* another."

"Ah, maybe being an attorney is *your* calling." Patrick buttoned his coat. "*Instead* of all this."

Constance nodded as she placed both empty glassed on the counter. "Maybe in my next life. I *enjoy* what I'm doing in *this* one."

Patrick reached for the door. "Ms. Ravine, I'll send some officers over tomorrow to take some statements from some of your staff. Maybe some of them could help us?"

"I'll talk to Mario. He handles scheduling for me." She closed the distance between them and stopped only a few inches from his face. The odor of the consumed alcohol, along with her natural attraction to him, made her shed the remaining shyness. "Do you have a card...or something?"

This girl exudes sex. Patrick stepped back. "Sure." He reached into his coat and handed her a business card. "The bottom number is my direct line. Give me a ring when it's convenient to talk to the staff."

He turned to exit but again stopped. He wasn't sure if it was the lack of sleep or if he had even heard correctly, but the mention of a man seeking two Asian females for a "party" picked at his brain. He turned back towards the casino owner. "Ms. Ravine, did you mention Collin Glover requested two women to accompany him the night of Azure Sutaki's death?"

Constance folded her arms across her chest. "Yes, I'm sure I did. Normally, he would just ask for Azure, but *that* night, he wanted two. I can make a quick call to find out who she was…if you need me to."

Hello? Of course I do. Patrick's eyes lit up. "I'd really appreciate it."

Constance picked up the phone behind the bar. "Just give me a minute or two."

Patrick nodded. He walked over to a window and watched as the snow had increased to almost whiteout conditions. The crowd on the street was all but invisible through Mother Nature's latest attack. Patrick's attention wandered back to Constance. He couldn't hear her from where he was standing, but the look of fear on her face was more than enough to tell him the news was not good.

The woman hung up and motioned for him. She handed him a piece of paper. "Detective, the other girl was Mikki Chax. The party service had her arriving *here* around 9:00 p.m., but she never reported back in for a scheduled birthday party the next night."

Shit. There could be two dead now. "Is this her address, Constance?" He lightly touched her on the shoulder.

Constance was shaking. "Yes. According to the party service, she lives on Hillside. It's just a mile or so from here."

Patrick rushed for the door, but her voice stopped him. "Detective, you don't think she's dead, do you?"

That or she skipped town. Patrick gritted his teeth. "I don't know, Constance…I *just* don't know."

CHAPTER TWENTY-THREE

New Haven's only elite auto dealership was in a state of peril. Hager Imports had been ravaged by the snow gods. Most of the inventory was covered with several inches, and Graneth Kensington, District Manager Extraordinaire, was in charge of making sure the vehicles were ready for the next business day. He had called in a skeleton crew to clear the pavements, but with only a few days until Christmas, other responsibilities pulled them away, leaving *him* to make the morning deadline. Considering the amount he already cleared, and his current pace, he *might* just make it.

No way for me to spend my after hours. Graneth pulled his scarf up around his face. The snow had dissipated some, but the wind was playing havoc in its aftermath. He tightened up the velcro on the gloves, then swiped the broom across the Mercedes' rear window.

The shrill sound from a parked car a few rows away surprised him and almost caused him to slip on a patch of ice. *Shit! Not now.* Graneth slammed down the broom. He plowed through the small drifts in the direction of the disturbance. A blast of cold air slapped him across the exposed part of his face.

"Damn," he cursed, almost falling a second time.

Stopping a few feet from the wailing, he took a quick look in both directions. Graneth decided the wind had set off the alarm. He peeked at his watch. *Damn, almost three o'clock in the morning.* It was later than he first imagined. Graneth knew he wouldn't even come close to finishing before potential buyers were filling the lot. *To hell with it.*

Discouraged, Graneth walked to the rear door of the dealership. As he stepped in front of the card reader, he noticed the small window adjacent to the keypad was flashing green. *Strange...I know it was locked.* He slid the access card along the reader, waiting for the light to flash red. After the alarm was reset, he stepped inside. *Glad nobody was here to see me fuck up.*

He jumped back. A loud scratching noise startled him. *Get a hold of yourself.* The car dealer had spent countless hours here on many occasions, mostly by himself, so the noises in this building didn't bother him.

Tonight, however, *something* felt different. The usual creaks and noises from the heater vents sounded unfamiliar. In fact, they were close to being on the verge of frightening. He stared up at the ceiling in search of the hot bright halogen bulbs. They usually gave him a headache, but right *now*, they would be a welcomed comfort. Graneth brushed some of the snow from his clothes. He reached for a knob on the wall and turned it clockwise. *Have some light in a few minutes.* A mechanical hum started to fill the room as the bulbs above started to flicker.

As he opened the door to his office, the aroma of chocolate filled his senses. He ripped off the scarf and threw it on the table. Graneth headed towards the desk and the object of his desire. *This will hit the spot.* He reached out and fingered the cellophane-wrapped plate. Graneth bent down, inhaling the sweet chocolate sensation. *Mum knows what I love.*

Graneth peeled the plastic away. His eyes were filled with excitement as he debated which treat to choose first. Satisfied with his choice, Graneth put the piece of chocolate back on the plate. He walked over to his portable fridge, then removed a bottle of wine. A quick peek at the year of its vintage, and Graneth was once again ready to truly indulge his lust for the finer things in life. He removed a corkscrew from his top drawer, making short work of the stopper, then grabbed a Hager Imports giveaway mug. Before he could pour the wine, something caught his eye. Graneth turned just in time to see one final flicker from the ceiling before the interior of Hager Imports was in complete darkness. Even the bank of security lights had been victimized.

Graneth dropped the mug. "Damn it to hell." He fumbled back to his desk, then for his top drawer. In the process, he bumped the plateful of treats. It smashed to the floor, pieces of chocolate bounced helplessly on the floor. "Wanker! Whoever is responsible is a complete wanker!"

He ignored the spill and located the receiver. He listened for a dial tone, but none was present. *Damn storm…cell phone in the car. Have to head that way.* Graneth fumbled some more until he withdrew a skinny metal object. He pushed the button, but nothing happened. He banged it on the desk, in hopes this action would provide a solution. To his amazement, the small bulb popped to life. A thin beam emerged through the lens. *Cheap asinine American flashlight.*

"About time!" Graneth yelled to no one particular.

He aimed the beam out the door but was unable to see anything beyond a few feet. The manager hesitated before he left the room, then turned back to grab something *else* off the desk.

A few steps later, he was confronted by finite blackness. The sliver of light helped guide him through the dealership. It was slow-going but first, but as his eyes got adjusted, Graneth closed in on the rear exit.

A few minutes later, he had reached his destination. "Finally." Graneth positioned the flashlight in front of the card reader. He groped inside his pants pocket until his fingers had grasp on the thin plastic. *One swipe, and I'm free.* Although he ran the card through, the display stayed dark. "Wanker!"

His first thought was to kick at the door and force his way out. He then realized, if the electricity was affected by the winter storm, the alarm system at the local police station would be going haywire right now. The police dispatcher would almost certainly send a few officers to ensure the dealership was free of undesirables. The winter storm would be a perfect opportunity for criminals to rape the establishment of its finer modes of conveyance. There wasn't any doubt that the local law enforcement didn't want to be responsible for *any* loss the dealership would incur.

Relax, the authorities will be here. Graneth tried the card reader once more but again was unsuccessful. He slumped against the door. *I guess I'll just wait here.*

* * *

Brandon Thornley had always been careful when it came to finding the right place to conduct his hobby. This *wasn't* the case when it came to dealing with Mr. Graneth Kensington. The man had turned him into the police, and *this* was about revenge. Up to this point, he had followed a *process.* A simple friend request on his favorite site, followed by choosing the select few who would see his dark side. *This* time he was playing it by chance. Brandon had clarity about who he was, and the realization of his thirst for blood was deeper than even he could control. *Case in point.*

There was no telling how long he could pretend to be *Brandon Thornley, Security Consultant* by day and evil-driven blood-seeker by night. Graneth's actions had resulted in law enforcement visiting him at *his* place of business. Brandon still wasn't convinced Detective Morgan hadn't noticed the makeup splotched across his face in haphazard fashion. *Probably break down my office door and drag me through the hallways like a common criminal.*

Brandon focused on his mission at hand. The Englishman was hunkered by the rear door. Brandon had short-circuited the dealership's internal security system, along with the phone lines. A few crossed wires here and there and he had bypassed the motion detectors. Brandon would return them to the proper settings once he had cast out his demons on the pathetic car dealer.

Brandon pulled down his black facemask. He unsheathed the knife. He stalked towards his prey, crouched like a lion in the midst of a hunt. *The police can't save you.* Reaching into his cargo pocket, he tossed the contents in the direction of Graneth Kensington. Several of the items bounced off the wall and scattered themselves throughout the hard tile.

Graneth jumped. "What in God's name?" He aimed the light at the floor.

Brandon smiled. *Just a few more steps*. He moved closer. The diversion seemed to draw Graneth's attention in the opposite direction from Brandon. *One more handful should do it*. Brandon adjusted his aim as he hurled the remaining objects to the other side of the room.

Graneth Kensington bolted to his feet. "Shit!" He scanned the floor with the light. He cocked his head as he bent down to examine on the objects. "What the hell are these buggers?"

Brandon leaped from his crouch, hitting Graneth between the solar plexus. The man was already in an awkward stance, so the force of the strike caused him to reel backwards, and the shift of weight was so great, it caused his ankle to snap in a compound fracture. The sound of crunching bone, followed by a blood curling scream, filled the dealership.

"Ah!"

Brandon smiled as muscle and bone were forced through Graneth's flesh. The Englishman tried to fight off his attacker, but Brandon was stronger. He held the man down with one hand, and placed the blade against his neck with the other.

Graneth whimpered. "My leg…why are you doing this to me?"

Show him who I am. Brandon pressed the steel flush against the Englishman's neck. Thin streaks of blood escaped from under the blade as he intensified the pressure. Brandon leaned in towards his victim. In one concentrated movement, Brandon severed his carotid artery. A cavernous trail of life juice was all that remained. Graneth Kensington emitted a few gurgling sounds as life ebbed away from him.

Do it now. Brandon removed the mask. A look of dismay, followed by one of acceptance filled, the face of the Englishman as his light was extinguished.

Brandon stared at the man for several minutes before he finally stood. Graneth Kensington *wasn't* going to join the others in *his* graveyard. Brandon had something very special planned for the man who had *betrayed* him. *Very special*.

CHAPTER TWENTY-FOUR

Too fucking cold. Donovan Petrie pushed the button on the Caprice's thermostat. He thought when the car alarm sounded *earlier*, the man would have spotted him, and *that* should have ended his night for spying on Brandon. But to his surprise, the man cast only a fleeting look in his direction before he turned and continued onward. That incident seemed ages ago, and Donovan hadn't seen the man since. He figured when he pulled the car up next to one of the dealership's imports, it would be a dead giveaway. Needless to say, with the fresh snow and dense visibility, he considered himself quite lucky.

The warm air was slow to exit the small heating vents. Donovan tapped at them, trying to circulate the flow. He shifted in his seat, then turned the interior lighting on just enough to read the digital display. *You gotta be shitting me.* Donovan knew it was *more* than past his time to abandon his surveillance. *Where the hell is Brandon?* He had witnessed his future victim park his Mercedes at the back of the lot. From there, Brandon walked towards the rear of the building. That was over two hours ago, and he *still* hadn't returned. *Can't risk staying here.*

Donovan checked his mirrors before turning on the engine. The wiper blades cleared a path on the windshield as he gently drove away from the dealership. Curiosity got the best of him. Donovan drove to the next side street and turned back in the direction of Hager Imports. If law enforcement happened to stop him, he could always *insist* he was looking for a new car. *Not a great excuse in this weather.*

Donovan entered the lot, careful not to drive too fast. Even though his adrenalin was surging, he tried to maintain his composure. *Brandon has to be around here.* He circled around back and noticed the only vehicle present was the snow-covered SUV he presumed to belong to the dealership employee. Donovan rolled down his window. The building had an overabundance of glass, but after close inspection, the interior appeared to be encased in darkness. *Where are the security lights?* He slowed the car to a stop and exited. Standing outside one of the display windows, he looked for any signs that Brandon or the salesman were still inside.

What the fuck? Donovan exhaled. The power to the dealership appeared to be lost. If he played Devil's advocate, the upswing was that the security cameras wouldn't have captured him on film. The downside was, Brandon Thornley may know someone was watching him, and *his* element of surprise was *now* compromised.

A loud bang came from behind him. Donovan spun around. *What's that noise?* "Someone here?"

Okay, I don't like this. He had the distinct feeling he was being watched. Donovan walked backwards all the way to his car. *I wonder?* He pulled it in gear and drove in the direction where he *hoped* Brandon Thornley was still parked. *Sly fuck.* He smiled. Brandon's Mercedes was no longer present. Donovan sat for a few moments before he picked up his cell phone. He wasn't sure if his new friend would mind him calling at this hour, so Donovan created an excuse.

The strong voice of Brandon Thornley answered. "Hello."

Donovan coughed. "Sir, sorry to bother you at home…but I'm a little under the weather today." *See if he buys it.*

Brandon laughed. "Well, too much work for you in your first week?"

This guy sounds too calm. "Nah, just spent some time shoveling the snow earlier. I don't think my dumb ass was ready for this damn blizzard."

"That's right…you haven't been in the Midwest long, have *you*?" Brandon joked.

He had to have seen me. "I guess not. Lesson learned, I suppose."

"No worries. Just make sure you're well before you come back…or I'll kick the shit out of you."

Acts like he's my best buddy. "Gotcha, by the way…what are *you* doing up? You like picked up on the first ring." *I'm very interested in that answer.*

"Oh, nothing too much. Working on expenditure reports for our investigative division."

At 0400? Yeah, right. "Better you than me, boss. Well, I'm going to get some rest. I'll be back tomorrow."

"Are you *sure* of that?" Brandon joked, then his tone turned serious. "Okay, just fucking with you. I'll see you tomorrow then."

"Yes, sir."

"Great. Let me get back to these reports." Brandon hung up without saying anything further.

I wonder why he was here? Donovan was more concerned with the reason his new boss had been less than forthcoming than paying attention to the police cruiser that seemed to appear out of nowhere. *Fuck me.* Checking the speedometer, it became obvious why. He eased the Caprice over to the side. The mixture of blowing snow and ice caused the car to end up in an awkward position. *Wonderful, probably will think I'm drunk, too.* Donovan's face turned red as he tightened his grip on the steering wheel.

* * *

Officer Amanda Hoskins was a welcomed addition to the New Haven Police Department. The twenty-five-year-old Iraqi War Veteran had only been with the department for six months, but already, she was working a patrol shift by herself and had earned respect from most of her peers. Even the senior leadership *knew* great things were in store for her. Officer Hoskins had been working on an accident report from earlier in the evening when the tan Caprice shot past her. She tossed aside the metal folder and activated her emergency lights. When the vehicle failed to acknowledge her existence, her pulse quickened with each passing second.

Officer Hoskins picked up the radio handset. "22-26 to dispatch."

A gruff smoker's voice answered. "Proceed with your transmission, 22-26."

"Dispatch, I'm south on Vista Road pursuing a tan Caprice. Iowa personalized plate, DEDIYD. *Weird ass signature.* It appears subject isn't going to stop." Her voice cracked.

"22-26, please advise if you need assistance at this time."

"Negative, dispatch. The driver appears to be pulling over. Looks like they are having trouble with the road conditions."

"10-4. Do you want us to hold the channel for you, 22-26?"

Officer Hoskins' voice lowered. "Negative, dispatch. I'll let you know."

"10-4," the gruff voice retorted.

Officer Hoskins exited the patrol unit. She unclipped her mini-flashlight from her belt as she cautiously approached. *Nice parking job, buddy.* The car had slid on a large, icy strip of road and was positioned almost sideways against the curb. She stopped short of the driver's side window but was able to tell it was a man behind the wheel.

"Sir, I'm Officer Hoskins with the New Haven Police Department. I stopped you because the speed limit is thirty-five in this stretch of roadway, and you were traveling approximately fifty miles per hour."

The man turned his head. "Really, I'm sorry. I didn't see the sign."

I hear that all the time. "I understand that, especially in these road conditions, but I still need to ask you for your driver's license, registration, and proof of insurance."

"Yes, officer. My registration and insurance card are in the glove box. May I retrieve them?" The man reached towards the glove compartment.

Something about this guy gives me the creeps. "Nice and easy please, sir."

The man chuckled. "Of course. Would hate to get shot *this* close to Christmas." He pulled out the papers and handed them to her.

You forgot something. "Sir…your license, please?"

"Sorry, I *think* I might have left it at home."

"Do you have any identification at all?" Officer Hoskins aimed the light further inside the vehicle.

The man shook his head. "Nothing. I'm really embarrassed."

Officer Hoskins scanned the paperwork. "Okay, Mr. Petrie. Let me check something out, and I'll get back with you in a few minutes."

"Anything you need."

She walked back to her patrol car and inspected the Caprice's license plate one more time. *Why does that look familiar?* She pushed a button mounted on the dashboard camera. *Better to see you with.* She radioed the dispatcher and relayed the information.

A few minutes later, the gruff dispatcher radioed back. A sound of urgency filled the small speaker "22-26. 22-26."

Something's up. "Go ahead, dispatch."

"22-26, be advised this particular vehicle was just reported by anonymous caller to have been involved in assault at Hager Imports. Also, be aware detectives have placed a description of this car on the *hit list.*"

I knew it. "10-4, dispatch. I don't have a cage in this car, so send me some backup."

"I'll send 22-18 in your direction now. Just got information from another dispatcher who talked to our caller…he has advised the man may be armed with a knife."

The plot thickens. "10-4, dispatch. I'll keep you posted."

Officer Hoskins monitored the video camera until she saw red and blue lights in her rearview mirror. After she brought the officer up to speed, they both approached Donovan Petrie's vehicle.

* * *

Donovan knew trouble was headed his way when the officer failed to return in an efficient time frame. The necessity for him to quench his curiosity had gotten him into this, and with the arrival of a second patrol unit, it *probably* wasn't going to end well. He peeked over his shoulder. *Shit. They're both coming.* After a quick survey of the car, he exhaled. *Nothing here to worry about.* He had been careful not to leave signs of his extracurricular activity *anywhere* inside the vehicle.

Donovan peeked over his shoulder. The female was approaching the vehicle on the left while another unidentified officer was coming from the right. *What the hell is going on?*

He heard the female officer yell in his direction. "Sir, I need you to exit the vehicle. Keep your hands where I can see them."

Are you fucking serious? Donovan pushed the door open and slowly climbed out. "What's this about—"

"Sir, turn around, and get down on your knees," Officer Hoskins raised her voice.

Be calm. They don't know anything. "Yes, of course. Whatever you say, Officer."

"Mr. Petrie, *you're* being detained for a reported altercation at Hager Imports, do you understand?"

Brandon did *see me there.* Donovan chuckled. "Huh? What kind of altercation are you talking about?"

"An assault, sir," Officer Hoskins nodded.

"What assault? I don't know what you're talking about."

"Sir, we received a report of a possible assault at the dealership which named you as the offender."

I just usually kill. Not so much on the maiming side. "This is a misunderstanding…really it is."

"Sir, we can discuss that once we check out the dealership, okay? Just bear with us."

No use arguing. Not the time or place. "My apologies. I understand you have a job to do."

The officers placed him in the rear of the patrol car as he waited for them to verify the assault had actually taken place. He wasn't sure how long he had been there, but it seemed *way* longer than it should have been. The rear door opened, and the frame of a large man appeared in the entryway. *Ah, this could be trouble.*

"Mr. Donovan Petrie. I'm Detective Patrick Morgan. I'm investigating several homicides in the metro area, and *I* think *we* need to talk..."

CHAPTER TWENTY-FIVE

Patrick Morgan stared through the two-way mirror. New Haven's prime suspect for all the recent slayings failed to offer himself as a sacrificial lamb, but to Patrick's surprise, he didn't avoid answering the questions poised at him, either. *He's crazy, or he didn't do anything.* The investigator was thumbing through a combination of sketches and colorful photos the crime scene investigators had provided and figured, if Donovan Petrie was involved, this *may* just push him in the right direction. Patrick was lost in thought when he was felt a tap on his shoulder.

"We don't have anything on him for the dealership, Morgan. A couple of uniforms checked it out. Nobody was there. Not *one* drop of blood at the scene, even if something *did* take place," Commander Cromartie said with a worn expression.

Patrick slammed the folder down. He wiped at his brow. "Even so, the vehicle he's driving *has* been witnessed at numerous crime scenes by several people...*including* Serena Owens and Aiden Jacobs. I can at least bring them in here—"

"About that, young man. Next time you send out an All Points on descriptors alone...you better check with me. For shit's sake...you didn't even have a partial plate number to refer to."

Patrick shook his head. "How many tan fucking Caprices are there, anyway? It was *right* to send this information out."

Cromartie pointed to a chair. "Sit your ass down. I don't care what you *feel* is right. I make certain decisions based on what evidence we have, Morgan. You *do* remember what evidence is?"

Please spare me a sermon. Patrick nodded. "Of course I do."

Cromartie pulled out another chair. His voice softened. "Look, I have no problem with you having those witnesses come down and take a quick peek at him, but take a *good* look at him,

Morgan." Cromartie pointed at the glass. "You think *he* could throw the girl off the roof? He would have a hard time punching his way out of a paper bag."

Well, he's right. Donovan Petrie didn't possess enough body strength needed to toss Azure Sutaki to her death. Patrick cocked his head. "I don't think he killed *her*."

"Have you found something else since you questioned him?" Cromartie leaned in.

Patrick removed his coat. "No. He's been willing to answer my questions, and I haven't uncovered anything."

Cromartie rubbed his chin. "Did he ask for an attorney or to make any phone calls?"

Patrick chuckled. "No. I asked him if he wanted legal counsel or if he needed to tell anyone where he was at. He looked at me, and said, 'I don't have anyone who cares about me, not since a long time ago.'"

"Okay, *you're* right. He's a little odd. Like I said, contact the two people who saw this guy, and we'll go from there. If nothing pans out, we cut him loose."

Patrick stood up. He glared at the colorless face of Donovan Petrie. *Even if Serena and Aiden can't put him at the scene, this is still a big a mistake to let him go.* He turned towards Commander Cromartie and sighed. "Whatever you say. Question for you, anyway. How many Caprices match what *he's* driving?"

Cromartie reached inside his jacket. He handed Patrick a piece of folded paper. "*That* many. A few years ago, the State Patrol auctioned off their entire stock of Caprices and Impalas. I'm surprised *you* don't own one."

Patrick frowned. "Okay, I got your point."

"Good."

Commander Cromartie opened the door. They started to exit when the office phone started to chip. Cromartie snatched it off the ringer. "Commander Cromartie."

Patrick couldn't hear the conversation, but from the expression on Commander Cromartie's face, he knew it was *something* important. A minute later, Cromartie hung up the phone. "You know who Mikki Chax is?"

Patrick nodded. His heart missed a beat. *The other stripper.* "Where?"

Cromartie zipped up his coat. "Girl just walked into Ravine's Goldmine. Constance Ravine is bringing her in."

"Sounds like she's finally coming out of hiding." Patrick held the door for his supervisor.

Cromartie managed a smile. "That's not all. This Mikki seems to remember what the killer looks like."

"About damn time we have something useful," Patrick said.

Cromartie held a hand up to quiet the younger investigator as he unlocked the door to the interrogation room.

Donovan Petrie was doodling on piece a paper. He looked up and grinned. "I guess if there are two of you, that means *one* of you is the good cop, and the other…will be playing the bad."

Arrogant fuck. Patrick's face turned red. "Mr. Petrie, just a little while longer, and we should be done."

Donovan shook his head. "No worries. I'm willing to fully cooperate with your investigation."

Cromartie adjusted his coat. "We appreciate the help. I just have a few things more to ask. Hopefully, *we* can clear this up, and *you* will be on your way."

Donovan leaned back. "I hope so. I don't want to miss work."

Patrick opened the brown folder that was tucked under his arm. "Ah, Langston Security Solutions?"

Donovan smiled. "That's what I told *you* earlier."

Patrick put up a hand. "I remember…but the Commander wasn't here with us then."

Donovan gave Cromartie a half salute. "Well, *Commander*, I told *him* earlier, I work for Brandon Thornley as a Threat Assessment Specialist."

Cromartie nodded. "I'm sure Mr. Thornley has thousands of capable applicants. You must have *something* to offer his team."

"Maybe I was just lucky," Donovan spouted.

"Perhaps, but I highly doubt it."

Patrick listened as Commander Cromartie fired questions at the thin man, but none of them even caused Donovan Petrie to bat an eye.

Soon after, the door to the interrogation room opened. A New Haven patrolman motioned for Patrick to step outside. He followed. The familiar figure of the sensual Constance Ravine stood at the end of the hallway. She was accompanied by a young Asian woman, who sat in a chair next to her. The woman's clothing was tattered, and her current physical appearance was also less than flattering. Several grayish colored splotches were strewn about her exposed flesh. Most were located in the face and upper arm region. *Out too long in the frozen temperatures.*

As Patrick walked towards the two, the girl clung to Constance Ravine. Patrick paused few feet away. "Hey, there. You must be Mikki. Ms. Ravine told me she was worried about you."

Mikki Chax looked up. "I see terrible things. Can't get out of my head."

Poor girl. "Mikki, I see you have some injuries."

Constance waved him off. "She was outside in that parking garage overnight. I have a doctor on staff at the casino. He treated her."

What don't you have on staff at the casino? Patrick nodded. "We will talk about that later." He moved closer to Mikki. "You and Azure were good friends?"

She covered her face. "My best friend. We do parties together." Tears flowed down both cheeks. "I so...sorry she gone."

"Hey...it's not your fault. Will you answer a few questions for me before we have you look at the man?"

Mikki eyes widened. She looked up at Constance Ravine for guidance.

Constance gave her an approving nod. "Honey, I think it would help."

Mikki shook her head. "I help you."

That's a start. Patrick had his notebook out. "Okay, you and Azure did parties together, right?"

Mikki smiled a little. "We did."

"Were you both going to entertain the night Azure died?"

"Yes." Mikki closed her eyes.

Patrick waited for her to open them before he proceeded. "Were you or Azure familiar with the person who hired you for the party?"

Azure looked up and to the right. She appeared to be trying to remember something. "I didn't. Azure knew man *very* well."

I'm sure of that. Patrick scribbled on the paper. "You wouldn't happen to know *his* name?"

Mikki shrugged. "Not really. Azure call him Glover-man. He like had lots of money, though."

Glover-man. Interesting name. "Lots of money, huh?"

Mikki smiled. "*Lots.* He drove us in *Jage-warr.* Is that how you say it?"

Patrick smiled. "Close enough. Did Glover-man buy you two any drugs or alcohol?" His eyes focused on Constance. *I know the answer to this question.*

Mikki bowed her head. "Glover-man gave us some white powder and a few special pills. I had a lot of Champagne...I think."

White powder and special pills. Hmm. "And you didn't get in on the party with those two?"

Mikki nodded. "No, they left me in car. I too happy; must have made me sleepy."

"So, you woke up and left the car?"

"Yes, I woke up and saw man grab Azure."

Excellent. "What happened next?"

Mikki wrung her hands. "I pass out. Woke up again, and nobody around. I left car to find Azure. I no find her."

Passed out while her best friend was murdered. Unbelievable. "So you just wandered around?"

"No. No clothes and still weak. I no want to go back...man might be there. I hide behind some cars to stay warm."

Hence, the frostbite. "Okay, so question for you?"

"Yes."

"Glover-man's car is still there?" Patrick poised his pen.

"Yes, I sure. I show *you* where."

One step closer, at least. "That would be very helpful." Patrick cocked his head. "Mikki, is Glover-man the person you saw grab Azure?"

Tears filled the corners of her eyes. "I no think so. I so...sorry Azure dead. I too drunk and happy to help. I sorry."

So am I. Patrick touched her arm. "Mikki, if the man knew *you* were there...you would be dead, too."

She wiped the tears from her face. "Ms. Ravine say him *here*. That true, Mr. Policeman?"

A gentle look filled Patrick's face. "I hope so. We aren't sure if this is him...*that's* why we need your help."

Mikki Chax swept a hand through her matted hair. "I do what you ask."

Patrick stood. "We have a room...over here."

Mikki's eyes widened as she tightened her grip on Constance Ravine's clothing. "No, I no want him see me."

Patrick soothed his voice. "He won't be able to. I promise. The room has a two-way mirror. He won't even know you're there."

Mikki loosened her grasp. "Promise?"

Patrick smiled. "Yes. Cross my heart." He swept his fingers over his chest.

Mikki moved slowly away from her benefactor. "Okay, I follow."

Patrick motioned for Constance to stay with the uniformed officer as he escorted Mikki Chax into the spacious room. A set of blinds covered the mirror. "You ok to do this?"

Mikki crossed her arms. "I ready."

Patrick flipped open the blinds. Commander Cromartie had left the area, and Donovan Petrie was sitting in the chair, still appearing to be in his worry-free state.

"Mikki, take a *real* close look. Do you recognize the man in the room?"

She stared at the man but said nothing.

Maybe shock has got the best of her. Patrick sat down next to her. "Mikki, did *he* kill Azure?"

She turned to face him. "I no understand…this not the man. I no see him."

Fuck me. "Are you sure, Mikki?"

Her body trembled. "I sure…the man…much larger." She pointed at Patrick. "Like you, Mr. Policeman."

Patrick rubbed the back of his neck. *Gonna have to let pale boy go.* "Thank you for looking, at least. If you give me a few minutes, we can go to where Glover-man's car is…if that's all right?"

Mikki smoothed out her thin dress. "Yes, but I scared he out there. I no want to die."

Patrick touched her arm. "We aren't going to let anything happen to you." He escorted her to the front door. "Officer Meehan will escort you to my car. Maybe you can describe what he looks so we can draw a picture of him."

Mikki managed a crooked smile. "I know what he look like."

Patrick nodded. "I just need a few minutes, and we can go."

"Okay." Mikki walked down the hall with Constance Ravine and Officer Meehan.

Patrick glared at the clock hanging above the doorway. His phone vibrated. Patrick stared at the text message in disbelief. *Not going to be able to hold him any longer.* Aiden Jacobs and Serena Owens were now out of the mix as well. The text he received told him Serena had moved out of state to live with family, while Aiden Jacobs had apparently run away. *What else could go wrong?* What scared him more than anything was the distinct possibility that Donovan Petrie wasn't involved in any of these homicides, and if *that* was truly the case, *someone* out there was waiting for another opportunity to kill again. Maybe there was a chance Mr. Glover-man was responsible for at least the death of Azure Sutaki. But chance was a game Patrick didn't enjoy playing.

CHAPTER TWENTY-SIX

Brandon Thornley was confident the neighbors of Collin Glover would have little compassion for the missing man, but he *still* implemented every safety protocol available as he returned for an encore performance. The realization that the dead man's Jaguar was present in the parking garage told him the police hadn't picked up on that lead...*yet*. He stared down at the pale skin of Graneth Kensington. *Too bad for you.*

Brandon's mind kept racing about the unwanted guest spying on him at the dealership. Just the thought of it alone had spooked him at *first*, but when he spotted the partially covered Caprice, a simple solution presented itself. The call to the dispatcher *was* risky. Brandon wasn't even sure if he was going to be able to sneak away, especially hauling the extra weight of his victim, but as *always*, he remained unscathed. The identity of the voyeur and why he was there at that time of night was interesting, to say the least. *Maybe we will meet again? But for now, back to work.*

Brandon had stripped off Graneth Kensington's clothing. The man was positioned in one of Collin Glover's expensive chairs. Brandon placed him upright in the middle of the room. *Now, we are ready.*

He picked up a brown folder and concentrated on *one* of the photos from the Jamie Brooks homicide. A few inquiries to former friends working at the crime scene, along with offering to donate a handsome sum of money to the dead girl's family, and *presto*, he was in possession of classified material. Brandon ran his hand over the color picture. Even though he considered *himself* to be skilled in the ways of murder, something about how this killer went about his work actually impressed him. Brandon studied it and recreated a likeness right in front of him.

One more thing left to do. Brandon kneeled down and inspected the candles. From his bag, he removed a book of matches. After he was satisfied everything was just right, he lit the candles. Brandon scanned the photo one more time before he stepped back from the kill area. *Almost perfect.* He closed the folder and stuffed it back from where it came. *You served a purpose, Englishman. A purpose, indeed.*

Brandon walked over to the breakfast bar to collect his personal belongings. He noticed a blinking light on his cell phone, then clicked the unlock button. His lips formed a slight grin as he read the message.

Hey, buddy. U working 2 day? I called the office and they said u were out.

Brandon typed.

Just a little work. Nothing too major. What's up?

Nada. Was a little detained earlier, but now free from sickness.

Brandon laughed.

I guess that means you'll be at work tomorrow.

All this white stuff on the ground you should have snow days.

Brandon shook his head.

No rest for the wicked...you know.

Lol. Oh, you have that so right.

Brandon gazed at the clock on the wall and thought, *Shit. Gotta get out of here.*

He typed in a few more words and hit the send key, then peeked at the time. Only had a few hour to get ready before it was time for his son's Christmas concert. Brandon shoved the cell in his cargo pocket. He scurried towards the front door and took one final glance at Graneth Kensington. *Good work.* Laughing, he shut the door behind him.

* * *

Donovan Petrie read the last message Brandon had sent. *I could kill him at his kid's concert.* An uneasy look covered his face as he pulled the dirty blinds open. The unmarked Tahoe had dropped him off at his apartment two hours ago, and he knew it wasn't a coincidence that *they* were still there. Donovan cherished the moment when he saw the reaction on Homicide Detective Patrick Morgan's face as he apologized for inconveniencing him. *Whoever* was behind the mirrored glass was unable to identify him as *the* sought-out killer, even though that's *exactly* what he was. Now, he was home to plot out the *next* step: to end Brandon Thornley's life.

Donovan was convinced Brandon *knew* it was him outside the dealership. What he *was* confused about had more to do with why Brandon had gone there. *There was a reason. Just need to find out a little more about Brandon.*

He booted up his laptop. A few minutes later, he was staring at Langston Security Solutions Executive Board. There had been substantial press about board members, but Brandon Thornley, without question, had the most. Donovan had been given special access to the secure site, but he was careful not to spend too much time in one area. Donovan discovered links to several articles as he scoured the database. *This is it.*

He double clicked the link. The screen went through a series of graphics before he was finally able to read the title of the piece. "The Balance Between Fortune and Family." A photo caption was below it. Donovan hit the *print screen* button as he perused the selection. It was actually quite intriguing. What really caught his attention was how Brandon Thornley had let the reporter who created the article delve into his personal life. *If Brandon was the security genius everybody envisioned him to be, he forgot one thing: never endanger your loved ones.*

Donovan snatched the paper from the printer, his heart racing as he scribbled a few notes on the back. *How perfect is this?* He would use the most precious commodity Brandon Thornley possessed to initiate the man's own demise. Donovan glanced at the screen and smiled, then minimized the article. He was still logged on to Langston Security Solutions secure page, so his search would be quick and easy. After scrolling through several screens, he saw a tab labeled *Personal Demographics.* A few seconds later, the information he needed printed out.

Reaching into a cubby hole on the side of his desk, he flipped open the calendar Langston Security Solutions had provided on his first day of employment. *Only a small window of time left, and the first phase of my agenda will be complete.*

CHAPTER TWENTY-SEVEN

The four-story parking garage at Chester and Vine usually housed the vehicles of the adjacent condominium owners. At the present, it was a command center for the New Haven Police Department. Patrick Morgan had been excited when Mikki Chax insisted she knew the exact location where Glover-man's vehicle was parked. That, however, wasn't the case. The compilation of the recent winter weather, plus the packed lot, had made it more difficult for the girl to remember. It all changed, though, when Patrick pulled onto the fourth-floor ramp. Mikki Chax's eyes filled with tears as the memories came flooding back to her.

Glover-man's Jaguar was on the opposite side of the ramp. The man had parked in erratic fashion, which would verify Mikki Chax's statement about him being in an impaired state. Patrick instructed Mikki to stay in the unmarked car as he approached. He remembered the driver's side door being ajar. That was *all* Patrick needed to see. Even though the snow was mostly covering the door handle, the recent sunlight had cleared enough for him to witness several dark splotches as they patterned themselves against the heavy steel. Patrick backed away and radioed for Crime Scene Investigators.

That had been over an hour ago. *Now*, he was in the process of locating Collin Glover. In normal circumstances, the license plate demographics would be reported to dispatch, and they would have the information back in a timely fashion. *Today*, it was much more difficult. The registration information returned to an address out of Caterville, which was a suburb east of New Haven. Several calls had been made to the phone number on file, but to this point, it had been a dead end.

Commander Cromartie stopped his vehicle next to where he was standing. "Morgan, where did your witness go?"

Patrick jerked his head. "She is with Tammy from Crisis Management Services. She said she can identify the killer, so Tammy will be with her and the sketch artist, once she's ready."

Cromartie looked in the girl's direction. "Once we go inside, we can radio for her. Just depends if Glover is *even* still around."

Patrick tugged at his sleeve. "If we can avoid exposing her to him, I want that done. Okay?"

"Good enough." He turned off the engine and exited. "What about this Collin Glover? You think he killed the Asian girl?"

Patrick leaned against the car. "Not very smart to leave his car at the scene, if he *was* involved."

Cromartie chuckled. "Damn guy is an ambulance chaser."

Patrick rubbed his hands together. "Already called the law firm. He was scheduled for a few days off. By the way, the same address on file as Department of Transportation."

Cromartie stepped to the concrete wall overlooking the street below. "How many condos in this area?"

Patrick shrugged. "Seventeen different companies own properties here. I sent officers out to speak with whatever managers they could find, but *this* close to the holidays, I doubt we even get half of them."

"Fucking bad timing." Cromartie shook his head.

No kidding. "Unless you're the bad guy." Patrick looked over the ledge to the pavement below.

"You thinking what I'm thinking?" Cromartie said, with a raised brow.

A true player. Patrick smiled. "Really wouldn't surprise me. Hell, his wife wouldn't have a clue he if had his own little bachelor hideaway. You know what…on second thought, I have an idea. It *might* be better than waiting for responses from these condo managers." Patrick unclipped his cell phone and dialed.

"Constance Ravine speaking."

"Ms. Ravine, this is Patrick Morgan. I really need your help."

"Detective Morgan, if I can…I will."

"You wouldn't happen to have Collin Glover's address on file, would you?" *Of course she does.* "We are at a standstill. Only address we can find is in Caterville."

"Hmm. I *know* we have an address to send him promotional material from the casino. Hold on a second."

Patrick hit the speakerphone option so Cromartie could listen in. *Gambling was an addiction. Probably kept it from his wife.*

Constance returned to the conversation. "Detective, the promo items are mailed to an address *here* in New Haven. 111 Chester Street, unit 3G. That's all I have."

I knew it. "Great. This is what we needed. Thanks, Ms. Ravine. *This* guy could be the one who killed Azure."

Constance's voice softened. "You really believe that?"

"It's the best lead we have received so far…I hope we find *something.*"

"So do I, Detective…so do I."

* * *

Patrick Morgan, Commander Cromartie, and several officers were positioned in the hallway outside of Collin Glover's clandestine residence. The everyday sounds, like a television or radio playing, were nonexistent. This made it eerie in itself. The addition of adding a possible killer to the recipe created a much more ominous setting.

Patrick knocked on the door. "Mr. Glover, New Haven Police. Open up, sir."

Damn. No answer. Patrick knocked again, this time with much more urgency. "Mr. Glover. New Haven Police. I need to speak with you, sir!"

Still no answer. Patrick eyed the others. He motioned for two officers to step to the forefront. The men were genetic examples of fitness, and the simple wooden door would cry for mercy when they decided to show their strength.

Patrick silently mouthed a command, and within seconds, the group was standing in the entryway. *What the hell?* The room, except for where they had breached, was blanketed in darkness. *It was the middle of the day.* Patrick removed his tactical light. He scanned the wall for a light switch. He flipped the switch on, but the interior remained dark. *Should have counted on that.*

He aimed the beam in the direction where he thought the windows would be. The glass appeared to be covered with a dark substance. Patrick motioned for the closest officer to investigate further. Within a minute, the team member radioed him. The glass had been painted over in black spray paint, so the alternative was the usage of their mini tactical lights. Soon, there was a display of dancing light beams bouncing in all directions of the interior.

Cromartie tapped him on the shoulder. He whispered, "Do you smell that? What the hell is it?"

Flowers? "I think its lilac. Over there." Patrick pointed to the center of the room.

Cromartie seemed to forget all tactical training as he raised his voice. "Is that him?"

Patrick walked closer. "Mr. Glover? New Haven Police here, sir." *The guy's not fucking moving.* Patrick hastened his step. "Sir, can you hear me?"

Cromartie nudged him, as he pointed. "What's on the floor there?"

The odor of lilac was now overpowering the two. *Candles? No, it couldn't be.* Patrick was close enough to recognize the figure and the irreparable damage that had been done to him. *Why is he here?* Patrick fumbled with his portable radio. "Morgan to CSI unit twelve."

A scratchy voice responded. "Go ahead, Detective Morgan."

"Bring your team up here to unit 3G. We need you."

"Roger that, sir. We will be *en route.*"

Patrick turned to Cromartie. "That's not Collin Glover."

Cromartie rubbed his face. "What do you mean that's not him?"

Patrick pointed to the man. "*This* is Graneth Kensington...the auto manager at Hager Imports."

"Him?" Cromartie stared at the naked, bludgeoned torso. "How do you think *he* got here?"

Patrick aimed the light on the floor. "What I want to know where in the hell Collin Glover is."

Cromartie aimed his flashlight at the rear of the Englishman. "Well, by the looks of the mixed barbwire and intertwined steel, Mr. Glover has definitely moved up to number one suspect."

And seeing this, how can I argue? "Something's different."

Cromartie flashed the light at him. "Huh? Morgan, are *we* seeing the same thing here?"

Patrick's eyes focused to the candles. "Think about it for a second. All of the other murders—and I *do* mean all—involve this *exact* same setting. Slashed throat, feet nailed to the ground, barbwire shackles, but *this* is different. I don't remember this nasty flowery odor. Do you?"

Cromartie scratched his head. "*That's* your evidentiary findings…the smell of lilacs? Okay, maybe the guy decided to add something new to his method for ritualistic killings."

Before Patrick could respond with a less-than-appropriate comment, the CSI unit arrived. Scott Gather was the team leader, and he looked the part. The man was lanky and the birth-control glasses warded off any potential woman having interest. Scott even had matching pocket protectors on either side of his tan jumpsuit. But through all of that, Scott was the *absolute* in the collection of evidence and DNA.

He called out to Patrick. "Sir, what's up with the lilac smell?"

Patrick managed a weak smile. "Scott, seems like our guy has changed up a little with his method of operation."

Scott flipped off his glasses in Clark Kent fashion. "What's with the lights, fellas?"

Patrick aimed his light at the spray-painted windows. "Guess the killer likes the dark."

Scott flashed the two investigators a grin. "That's not all. The temperature in this room is *way* too cool." He motioned towards the thermostat. "You guys didn't notice it?"

Patrick and Cromartie stared at each other with ignorance. "We *were* outside, Scotty."

"The average temp for a place this size should be close to seventy degrees. It's fifty-three, according to this. Look where he placed the body."

Patrick nodded. "The middle of the room."

"Yes, but look where." Scott pointed up at the air vents.

Bastard did it on purpose. "He was trying to slow down the decomposition process." Patrick looked in the direction of the windows. "So, he also covered the glass to keep it cool."

Scott smiled. "And *they* say cops aren't too bright."

Patrick frowned. "Scott, like I told the Commander, something's not right about those candles. I'd like you to bag them and run a complete set of tests on them."

Cromartie turned away. "You and those damn candles."

Scott ignored the senior investigator. "Gotcha." He walked over to the corpse. "Who is he anyway?"

"English car dealer named Graneth Kensington. I actually interviewed him the other day." *Now, he's dead.*

Scott made a cross with his two index fingers. "*Please* never interview me then."

Patrick chuckled. "Just for forensic testimony."

"Of course," Scott said as he pulled out a set of purple latex gloves. He opened his evidence kit and withdrew four plastic bags. Each candle and its holder were in a separate bag. He stowed them inside a secondary compartment of the evidence kit.

Patrick shook his head as he pulled Cromartie off to the side. "The All Points is already out on Glover for the Azure Sutaki homicide. I'll add this to the alert, as well."

Cromartie stared at the dead man. "Good. I think it's safe to say it looks like Glover is *our* serial killer."

Or a copycat making him the scapegoat. Patrick wasn't about to mention that, so he just gave Cromartie a casual nod of confirmation as they discussed about the nuances of an impending press conference. It would ease the souls of citizens residing in New Haven to finally have a suspect identified in the brutal slayings.

Patrick appeared to be attentive to what his supervisor was saying, but a bevy of questions kept flashing through his head. The most intriguing had to do with Brandon Thornley. Was the well-respected corporate genius involved in the death of Jamie Brooks or Graneth Kensington? It *could* have been a coincidence, Thornley being spotted on the grounds of the abandoned church. *Hell,* he owned it. But the auto dealer's death was nagging at every inch of Patrick's body. Just a few days after Patrick was questioning the man about Thornley, *he* turns up *here*, murdered in ritualistic fashion. That was just too much for Patrick to swallow. *Too much...*

CHAPTER TWENTY-EIGHT

Brandon Thornley couldn't help but concern himself with his latest act of vengeance. The assassination of Graneth Kensington had been a knee-jerk reaction on his part. Brandon's sole existence was to remain hidden in the light versus spotlighting his kills for the public. The addition of his unknown admirer at the auto dealership had certainly complicated his plans. *At least for now.*

Brandon pushed through the doors of Langston Security Solutions, catching a glimpse of himself in the reflective glass. He ran his fingers over the scab of the wound Azure Sutaki had given him. *A reminder of my mistake*, he thought, hurrying by the security desk. When he turned in to the hallway, his second-in-charge, Monty York, spotted him and waved a paper in his direction.

"Boss, you're not gonna believe this!"

"What's going on, Monty?"

"They identified the killer in all those crazy murders."

Must have worked...for now. "Really? Who are they naming?"

Monty thrust the paper out towards him. "Look. I think you know him."

More than you think. Brandon grasped the paper. "Thanks." Brandon's gaze was draw to the bold printing.

New Haven Police Identify Suspect in Recent Homicides.

Brandon read the first few lines. A thin smile crossed his lips when Collin Glover's name appeared before his eyes. *Scapegoat, indeed.* A review of the article's content suggested local law enforcement were satisfied that the local attorney was the *only* suspect. Brandon's face lit up when he read that. He must have been too engrossed in the paper because Monty was waving a hand in front of his face, looking concerned.

"You all right?"

"Oh...of course." Brandon handed the paper back to him. "It's wonderful the animal has been caught."

Monty pointed at the article. "Well, he's been named as the suspect. *They* haven't found him yet."

Yes, they did. "*You* know what I mean...the city can have some peace before the holidays."

"Yeah, the son-of-a-bitch is lucky I didn't get my hands on him." He balled up both fists. "If I was still on the department—"

That's it. "Monty, you mentioned knowing several people there, right?"

Monty unclenched his hands. "Well sure, boss. Why? You need something?"

A very valuable something. Brandon motioned for him to move closer. "I think *someone* is following me. I need a little favor."

Monty tapped him on the shoulder. "If you have a stalker, boss, I think it should be reported—"

Brandon held up a hand. "Not yet. I want to keep it quiet."

Monty shook his head. "I don't agree, but I understand. What can I do?"

"Actually, it's something small. The person who is following me...I think drives a light colored Caprice—"

"Like the state patrol model?" Monty asked.

"I think so. He was tailing me the night of the snowstorm."

Monty frowned. "Boss, lots of those driving around the state. You sure it was a Caprice?"

I do pay attention to detail. "Sure of it. I just need to check and see if any patrol units stopped one the night of the storm."

Monty shrugged. "That's all?"

"I told you it was small." Brandon smiled.

"Just the plate information, then. Got it." Monty flashed a devious smile. "You're going to pay him a surprise visit?"

A surprise it will be. Brandon returned the smile. "Nothing too dramatic. Just an inquiry of sorts."

"I gotcha." Monty looked at his watch. "Give me about an hour. I'll let you know."

Brandon shook his hand. "Great! I *know* I can always count on you, Monty."

Monty beamed. "Means a lot...you saying that." The man reached out and shook Brandon's hand with such force his fingers started to turn white.

Brandon broke his grip. "So, within the hour then?"

"If not sooner." Monty waved as he walked down the hallway.

A few minutes later, Brandon was in his office, sitting at his desk. He logged onto *Konnect2u* and browsed his new messages. They consisted of the usual, like professors requesting his appearance at various educational institutions around the country to discuss security management. Brandon typed a few replies, but the urge to click on the list of friend requests was too tempting. He scrolled through the list until one in particular caught his attention.

The woman appeared to be in her mid twenties. Her dark complexion and her braided hair gave her a quite an exotic look. *This is the one.* Brandon scrolled through her profile. *Truly nice.* He clicked on the approval button as chills surged through his body. Monique Quentin was only a few hours from New Haven. *Perfect choice to end the year.* Brandon decided Monique Quentin *needed* to be the last conquest for a while at least. Especially if someone was keeping close tabs on him. The wound on his face should remind him of that. Another mistake, no matter how small, could prove to be devastating, and more than *that*, he would be exposed for *who* he truly was. His family would be dissected by the community. They would never escape the media frenzy that would most surely come.

Brandon glanced over at the picture of his youngest son. He turned away, just in time, to see an incoming text on his phone.

Hey, what's up, boss?

Just typing away. Aren't I paying you to work?

LOL.

Meet me in the parking garage after work. We're going to eat some steaks...my treat.

Tempting. Can't though. Some of us have only a few days left of Xmas shopping.

You sure? I heard about this great place.

Donovan, I really can't. Tomorrow is only half day...you want to then?

Sure. See ya then.

Btw...get your ass back to work.

LOL.

Brandon turned towards his computer. He brought up the information page on his newest project. Monique Quentin worked for a private research facility. Her daily posts on *Konnect2u* featured links to the company web site. After a few minutes, he had the location of her employer and started to map out a plan. Brandon was lost in the excitement of planning her demise when he heard a knock his door.

Brandon minimized the screen. "Enter."

Monty York frowned as he stepped through. "Boss, got your information."

Brandon's brows knotted. "What's with you?"

Monty reached into his pocket. He withdrew a folded envelope. "It's in here." He slid it over to Brandon.

He's acting strange. "Can't be *that* bad."

Monty pulled out a chair. "It's fucking *not* good."

The "f" word. I don't usually hear that kind of language from him. Must be something. Brandon peeled it open. His jaw dropped as he flipped the yellow document on the desk. *Why him?*

He looked up at Monty. "Okay, this is our secret. Your dispatcher friend is trustworthy?"

Monty's face turned red. "Yes. I couldn't believe it was him?"

A surprise to say the least. "Monty, I'll handle this. Could be easy explanation."

Monty stood up. "I'll tell you something…I didn't trust the guy since I first saw him, anyway. Looks like a damn vampire."

Brandon nodded. "You don't need to worry about it. I do have some experience in dealing with *this* sort of thing."

Monty chuckled. "I know…just pissed me off when I saw his name."

Me, too. "Just finish the shift. Half-day tomorrow. It'll be addressed before then."

"Okay, I'll back off." Monty opened the door. He shook his head as he walked out of the office.

Brandon fingered the yellow print-out. He clicked on the small box, which brought Monique Quentin into view. *She* would have to wait to join her place among his chosen. Right now, there was someone *else* who had just moved to the front of the line.

CHAPTER TWENTY-NINE

Donovan Petrie knew time was of the essence if his plan was to succeed. The New Haven Airport was the perfect place to conduct his search. Donovan walked along the sidewalk adjacent to the terminal. He noticed several limousines lined up along the curb. Each driver stood in front of their respective vehicles as they waited for their intended party. *This is the place to start.*

Donovan walked up to the first driver and, after a few minutes of idle chitchat, determined he didn't have the information Donovan needed. He repeated this process with each of the drivers for about an hour. Just as he was about to abandon his effort, he spotted someone he recognized as driver who would frequent Langston Security Solutions.

Donovan waved to the man. "Excuse me. Can you help me?"

The man looked to be in his mid fifties. The salt-and-pepper hair gave him a most distinguished appearance. He smiled when Donovan approached. "Hello, sir. How may I assist you?"

Donovan pulled out his identification. "I'm Donovan Petrie with Langston Security Solutions. I'm looking for a driver who is assigned to our security director. I wasn't sure if the chauffeurs hang out together, but it's important I find him."

The man laughed. "Son, *we* talk shop like any other profession. You said Langston Security Solutions, right?"

Donovan handed him a card. "I did. If you have any idea who the guy is, I would really appreciate it."

The man thought for a second. "Well, Mr. Petrie, I think the driver's name is Landon Tewes." He stuck his hand out. "By the way, I'm Peter Greensburg. I also drop off clients to your business all the time."

I thought so. "Great, here's the deal. I'm going to throw a little Christmas party for some of the executive board tomorrow night, and I need to get a hold of Landon to coordinate. I don't want Brandon to find out...if you know what I mean?"

Peter expelled a hearty laugh. "*That* kind of party, huh?" He reached into his trench coat and handed Donovan a business card. "Here you are. This should have everything you need. If your company *ever* needs another driver, keep me in mind."

Donovan handed an envelope to the man. "Peter, thanks. Just a little something for your trouble."

"No trouble at all. Do me a favor, though."

"Sure."

Peter smiled. "When you get a hold of that old bastard Landon, wish him a happy holiday, and tell him to give me a ring. It's been too long since we chatted and had a beer."

It's going to be even longer. "I'll do that. Again...thanks for helping me out. Tomorrow will be a day to remember."

Peter waved, as Donovan walked in a hurried pace towards the short-term parking lot.

* * *

Father of Faith was an exceptional education institution. The enrollment process was more similar to one of collegiate standards than it was for students just starting the learning process. The average applicant wouldn't even be considered for a reservation unless a generous monetary donation accompanied the child's application.

Ryan Thornley's parents would never admit it, but *he* was the benefactor of his father's success. He *knew* the teachers didn't consider him one of Father of Faith's gifted, and they didn't try to mask their disdain. On several occasions, while eating lunch, he would hear the staff making "fat" jokes as they passed by. The other children heard the conversations as well, and as *sometimes* kids do, took it upon themselves to make his life at the school a living hell. He had told his parents, but when his mother made an unexpected visit to the vice principal's office, the man had denied any wrong doing and blamed the behavior on the other kids, *not* the teachers.

Well, that was then, and *now*, he was just waiting for class to end for the Christmas break. Ryan stared at the wall clock. He tapped his pencil on the desk as excitement built up inside him. Mrs. Baines looked up from her desk. She cast a glare in his direction, which warned him to stop the commotion or face her wrath. Ryan put down the pencil. *It was going to be great*. It would be three whole weeks without the mean Mrs. Baines and the others who made fun of him. He would have Mom, Dad, and Sean, his older brother from college, around. They *never* made fun of him...*ever*.

As the hands of the clock came together at twelve, the bell sounded. Ryan threw on his coat and rushed out of the classroom. He burst out the front door and skipped over several of the brick steps on his way to the front sidewalk. The teachers were already positioned on the sidewalk, standing by to ensure the kids were being picked up. *Where is he*? Ryan looked up and down the street in search of his father's company driver. *I hope he's coming soon*. He stood there for a few minutes until one of Father of Faith's spiritual leaders walked up to him.

"Ryan, is everything okay? Where's your driver, son?

Ryan shrugged. "Must be late, Father Scanlan."

He touched Ryan's shoulder. "You want me to wait with you?"

Ryan shook his head. "Shouldn't be long, sir."

He looked up the street. The limo just turned the corner. It stopped several feet from the curb. Father Scanlan smiled at Ryan as he opened the door and got in. The car pulled into traffic. Ryan watched as the driver began driving a different direction than normal.

He pushed the intercom button. "Landon, we not going home?"

"Landon couldn't make it today. I'm his replacement, *Donovan*. Your dad is waiting for you."

Wow! Time with Dad. "Cool, is Mom with him?"

"No, just him. Mentioned he wanted to take you shopping for your mother's present."

Ryan smiled. "Well, Donovan, it's a pleasure to meet you."

"No, Ryan, the pleasure is *all* mine…"

CHAPTER THIRTY

Detective Patrick Morgan had been gazing at the bloody pictorial on the bulletin board for several hours. He was still not convinced Collin Glover was the primary suspect in the slayings. Commander Cromartie had issued a national pick-up order on Glover, so hopefully within a matter of days, the wanted man would be in custody. Patrick would be able to interrogate him, and he could get the answers he was searching for. He grabbed a folder from the desk, then removed the pictures and tacked them to the board.

Most of the photos had the same characteristics, but *one* was strangely dissimilar. Commander Cromartie had been too eager to wave off the *obvious* differences of Graneth Kensington's murder. The killer turning on the air conditioner; painted the windows black; and finally, used the fragranced candles. Why would Collin Glover all of a sudden change this many details? Those were the questions that plagued him all day, and it didn't seem to register with his supervisor or *even* his boss. Patrick *knew* the Chief of Police and Cromartie wanted to close the book on these *Holiday Murders*. This is what Chief Remmers had appropriately named them when he spoke with media earlier in the day. The citizens were assured by their leader that the rash of murders was finally solved. *I hope that makes everyone feel better.*

Commander Cromartie gave Patrick the ceremonial bullshit speech about how his skills in the investigation lead to Collin Glover. He instructed him to go home and spend some time with his family and *even* had the nerve to mention how Kelsey's medical condition was taking its toll on his work performance. Patrick would make sure to spend quality time with his family but *not* until he was certain this case was *over*. As far as *he* was concerned, he hadn't figured out *anything* yet. Patrick sat studying the forensic reports of each murder until he heard a soft knock at his office door.

Dr. Abbey Krieger stepped inside. "Hello, Detective. I have been trying to get in touch with you or the Commander for a few hours."

Patrick rubbed his eyes. He unclipped his cell and realized the battery was dead. "Shit, I'm sorry. I have been here since 3:00 a.m.; must have forgot to charge it." *What was the point? The case was over according to everyone else.* "The Commander probably turned his off, with the murders being solved and everything," Patrick scoffed.

"Solved?" She pulled off her white ski jacket. "I wanted you to see this." She handed him a black folder. "The autopsy of Graneth Kensington."

The fatigue left Patrick in a hurry. "You found something?" He rifled through the paperwork.

Dr. Krieger sat next to him. "I wasn't sure at *first*, but after I did some blood work, I knew something was off."

Patrick cocked his head. "What do you mean?"

Dr. Krieger leaned closer. "Look towards the back. I usually take just one or two pics for identification purposes, but this is interesting." She pointed at two snapshots.

Patrick stared at them. "Looks like our killer stabbed him *before* he slit his throat."

Dr. Krieger tapped the first photo. "This wound *here*, Detective, created more than enough damage to do the job." She then pointed to the other. "This wound to the lungs was done *post-mortem*."

He inflicted more damage after? Patrick slumped in his chair. "Double the work with the same return?"

"Not exactly." She turned to the second page of the file. "If you look *here*, the blood work tells you all."

Holy shit. "Is this right?"

Dr. Krieger tapped at the paper. "Blood doesn't lie. Mr. Kensington had been dead for twenty-four to thirty hours before *you* found him." She let that soak in before she continued. "You *also* need to know, the wound pattern to Kensington's throat is different than *all* of the others."

Did this mean? Patrick shot up from his chair. "Are you saying what I think?"

She flipped back to the photo of Kensington's severed throat. "The person responsible for *this* has training in the *art* of killing. The cuts on the others don't *even* come close in comparison. They were done in an angry and chaotic fashion."

Not a discipline law school is known for. Patrick pointed to the bulletin board. "Not so solved, is it?"

* * *

Patrick Morgan sent a fax to his supervisor highlighting the medical findings Dr. Krieger had documented. He left the office and headed to the one person he *knew* had information that could lead him in the right direction. Mikki Chax had left the police station before the sketch artist could get a description of the man who killed her friend. Patrick double-checked the address she had given to the desk officer. He honestly couldn't blame the girl for wanting somewhere she would feel safe, but given the circumstances, Ravine's Goldmine wasn't first on *his* list for an acceptable sanctuary. Patrick was well aware this girl *was* the key to the investigation.

Constance Ravine seemed pleasantly surprised when she met him at the foyer to the casino. "We have the habit of crossing each other's path...though I can see by your expression this *isn't* going to be a social visit."

This woman had nerve. "No, I need to find Mikki. She left the other day before we could get a sketch."

The smile on Constance face turned into one of disgust. She pulled him to the side. "You are fucking unbelievable! *That* young girl has been through a whirlwind of emotions the last few days...why are *you* doing this to her?"

"The man who killed Azure is *still* out there, Constance. I need anything she can give us—"

A bewildered look replaced her anger. "What? The news said Collin Glover was the murderer...*he* wouldn't come back here."

I don't have time for this. "If *you* remember, Mikki told us it *wasn't* Collin Glover who killed her friend. Anyway, with the information I got earlier, *I* need her help to find out who it *really* was."

Constance shook her head. "Why would the police say *he* was responsible when he wasn't?"

"My bosses *will* have a new perspective tomorrow, but *right now*, I need *you* to take me to Mikki."

She led him to a private elevator. "She's upstairs in one my guest rooms." Constance turned to walk away but motioned for Patrick to follow her. "I'm going with you."

Don't argue. "Lead the way."

The elevator emptied into the hallway adjacent to the private quarters of Constance Ravine's special guests. She escorted him around the corner. She stopped at the first door to her right and knocked on the door. "Mikki, you in there?"

"Yes, Ms. Constance. You need me?"

Constance pushed open the door. "Honey, someone needs to see you."

Mikki Chax was stretched out on the king-size bed. She curled up in a ball when she saw Patrick in the doorway. "I know you mad at me...but I afraid to stay *there*...so I go."

"Mikki, I'm not upset. I just came to ask you for your help."

Mikki sat up. "You no mad?"

Patrick managed a smile. "No, *I* just want to catch the man who killed Azure."

Mikki bowed her head. "I very much like *that,* too."

Patrick slowly walked towards her. "Hey, I have an idea. Instead of *you* going to the police office, how about if *I* have my sketch guy come here?"

"I like that better, Mr. Policeman, but I do draw him already." Mikki smiled.

Huh? Patrick thought his ears were playing tricks on him. "Mikki, *you* have a picture of him?"

She reached over to the wooden dresser. Opening it, she pulled out several pieces of folded paper. "*His* face makes me not want close my eyes. Please take them…maybe they help you."

"Thanks," Patrick unfolded them. *Amazing!*

The girl had substantial talent, which would propel her from Constance Ravine and the XXX parties that had put her in this mess in the *first* place. Patrick flipped through the pictures. Each had a few differences, but one thing remained constant. The man had a dark mark on the right side of his face. The size and shape was *always* the same. *Why is this so familiar?* He pointed to the mark. "Mikki, can you explain to me what *this* is?"

Mikki leaned over him. She motioned with her hands. "Man cut…he bleed."

A wound. It was a wound. Patrick stared into the man's features. Whoever he was, the man had been injured at the scene of *his* crime. Azure Sutaki had made sure her killer would have *something* to remember her by. Patrick recalled Dr. Krieger saying the DNA from under Azure's fingernails was very difficult to process, and a match so far, hadn't been identified. But if the killer was still bleeding when he grabbed her by Collin Glover's Jaguar, the CSI team *should* have another sample of blood available for testing. Patrick stuffed the drawings in his jacket. He thanked Mikki and Constance before rushing back to his vehicle. Patrick dialed a number on his cell phone as he sped out of the parking lot. There was *only* one other person *he* knew skilled in the art of forensics and blood collection. And *he* was on the way to visit him.

CHAPTER THIRTY-ONE

Brandon paced the living room, glaring at the grandfather clock in the corner. *Ryan should have been here by now.* The driver usually had the boy home on time, but today, he was already an hour late. That wasn't the *only* thing on his mind though.

Brandon flipped open the liquor cabinet. He clenched his teeth as he took a sip of vodka from his glass. His number *one* problem was Donovan Petrie. The asshole had been following him, and given what Brandon did in *his* off time, there was no telling how much the man had witnessed. Donovan had cajoled him from the start. The answer why had not been unveiled, but *he* would make sure to ask before he buried the man under the earth.

Brandon picked up the cordless and dialed.

"Father's of Faith Elementary School. This is Jill. How may I help you?"

"Jill, this is Brandon Thornley…Ryan's father. I thought the students were releasing early today?"

"Mr. Thornley, they were let out over an hour ago. I'm in the office and don't see anyone in the waiting area."

Something's not right. "Jill, are any of the teachers around…and if they are, would you check? *Maybe* Ryan is outside on the playground?"

"Sure, Mr. Thornley. Give me a few minutes, and I'll get back to you." The girl's voice was replaced with the sound of holiday music.

Check with Carina. Brandon grabbed his cell phone from the table.

Two rings later, his wife picked up. "Hey honey, what do I owe this pleasure?"

"Carina, did Ryan say anything about staying after class today?"

"Hmm, I don't think so. I thought by now you two would be setting up the house for *our* Christmas Eve party."

Shit. Almost forgot about that. "No, I was waiting for him. Do me favor. I'm on the other line with his school. Would you call the limousine service to see if they picked him up?"

"I will. Brandon...you think something happened? Maybe an accident?" Her voice was nervous.

"Don't start thinking like *that*. Just give them a call and let me know...okay?"

"I'll contact them now," Carina said in almost *too* soft of a tone. She disconnected from the call.

Brandon picked up the cordless. The music was still playing, so he knew Jill hadn't returned. Within a few minutes, she was back.

"Mr, Thornley. Ryan was picked up just a *few* minutes later than usual today."

Where is he then? "You're sure?"

"Yes, he's gone from the campus, sir."

Brandon slammed the cordless back on its base. Several white chunks of plastic broke away and bounced onto the carpet. *Ryan, where the hell are you?* As a leader of men, Brandon was able to solve almost any problem that came his way, but for the first time in his life, he felt powerless. *This* time, someone *else* was in control. He gripped the cell phone with both hands, hoping his wife would call and verify his son was fine, but when he saw her burst through the door, he became nauseated.

Carina explained the dispatcher for the limousine service had confirmed Ryan had been picked up at his regular location, but the driver hadn't been in contact since. Brandon decided it was time to contact the police. Even though he thought it was poetic justice in its truest form to have the police nosing around a serial killer's house, it was his *only* chance to find Ryan. Brandon had taught *both* his son's to be mindful of their surroundings. He knew Ryan wouldn't willingly go with a stranger, but Landon *wasn't*, and he honestly seemed to be a stand-up type of person. Of course, Brandon realized that was what most who came in contact with *him* also thought...and how wrong were *they*?

The police dispatcher took down the information. She ensured Brandon an investigator would be on scene within a short time. After just a few minutes of waiting for the police, Brandon heard whimpering from the adjoining room. He peeked into the kitchen. Carina Thornley was huddled in a chair. Her eyes were damp with tears, as she held the phone tightly against her chest.

Carina looked up when she saw Brandon in the doorway. "Where is *he,* Brandon?" She wiped at her face.

Brandon knelt down next to her. "We'll find him...I *promise*." He caressed her face with the back of his hand.

Carina reached out and took his hand in hers. "Why is this happening to *us*?" She sobbed even louder.

Because bad people roam the earth. I should know. I'm one of them. Brandon shook his head. "I don't know." He gently took the phone from her. He walked towards the rear of the house so Carina wouldn't hear him. Brandon hit the speed dial button.

"Hey, boss," Monty York answered.

"I need a favor." Brandon voice was shaky.

"You sound like shit...what's up?"

"Ryan's missing. The limo driver picked him up from school a few hours ago but hasn't returned or called us."

Monty's voice lowered. "Damn, I'm sorry...you think he wants a ransom?"

Brandon sighed. "Maybe...but I'm not getting that vibe. If you know who has experience in this. I need them." *Wow, that's ironic.*

"Boss, give me ten minutes. I'll shake someone down in Missing Persons. We'll figure it out."

"Thanks, partner."

That driver will be sorry he ever met me. He ended the conversation. He stopped at the kitchen door. His wife was still seated in the chair, but *this* time, she didn't even look up when he entered the room. *Carina doesn't deserve this pain.* Brandon started to approach her, but the vibration of his cell phone stopped him. *Something about Ryan.* His fingers trembled as he fumbled with the device. His sudden hope vanished when he realized it was *just* a text from Donovan.

Happy Christmas Eve, buddy.

Don't have time to chat right now!

Something wrong?

Family emergency.

Ah, I would it call it something else.

Brandon stared at the display. *That makes no sense...unless...* Beads of sweat formed on his face as his pulse quickened. He punched out a few words.

What would you call it then?

The display lit up.

More like a very tragic ending...yes, I think that's a perfect way to describe YOUR situation.

Oh my God, this is why he's been following me, Brandon thought. His face turned flush. He tapped at the keys with fury in his eyes.

You have Ryan?

Good guess...maybe you should call the cops.

I already did. Now, I know you have him it won't be long.

Ha ha! If you mention my name, Ryan won't have long.

His mind swirled. *Fuck, what do I do?* Brandon stared at his wife. She was still in a state of shock. *Gotta be sure first. Can't take his word for shit.* He typed several words and waited for the response. Then it came, and like *all* bad news does, it hit him with full force and without mercy.

Black winter coat, white shirt, black tie, and black pants.

Brandon's eyes filled with wetness as he remembered Ryan leaving the house in that *same* attire. He then turned and ran upstairs. Opening his closet, he pulled out *his* brown pouch of tools. Donovan Petrie had made a *serious* miscalculation if he thought kidnapping Ryan was going to be financially rewarding. Brandon reached in and freed one of his blades. It felt comforting as he ran his fingers along the serrated edge. He grabbed the sheath and attached it to his belt.

Brandon reached into his night stand and removed the stainless steel Mazre .40 caliber handgun. This *wasn't* his style, but Donovan had proven to be a *worthy* adversary. This was evident by how effortlessly the man had been in ripping his son away from him. Brandon shoved the gun in his trench coat. He typed another message. A few minutes later, Brandon was in the Mercedes and on the way to save his son. *If you want to play...play we shall.*

CHAPTER THIRTY-TWO

Patrick Morgan pushed the number four on the elevator panel. A mass exodus ensued once the door slid open. *This* floor housed the laboratories of the county's forensic staff. They had been working non-stop collecting and processing evidence in the *Holiday Murders*, so when Collin Glover was named as the prime suspect, it was like music to their ears. Supervisors of the team *all* agreed: a few days with family and friends would be just what this group needed. *At least someone was in the Christmas spirit.* Patrick weaved his way through the winding hallway until he finally reached his destination. He pushed the intercom button and waited.

"Welcome to forensic world. You bag 'em, and we do all sort of nasty stuff sorting out *who* killed 'em." Scott Gather's voice cackled.

Guy has some sick humor. The lock on the door disengaged. Scott was behind a large elongated steel table. He was organizing several stacks of beakers and almost dropped a few when he saw Patrick. "Damn, I drop those, and Big Brother *will* cancel my birthday."

Maybe he's a little crazy. "Not before you *first* help me."

Scott pointed at him. "Ouch, that hurt the only feeling I had left." He finished putting the glass tubes away before he approached Patrick. "Hey, after you called, I went back through my logbooks of what was collected at the Azure Sutaki murder."

"Anything?" Patrick asked.

Scott smiled. "You know me, *I* always find *something*."

He led Patrick through a series of doors and into another laboratory even larger than the one they just left.

Patrick shook his head in disbelief. "Little mad scientist seems to have a healthy budget."

"I spare no expense at the cost of *my* employer." Scott winked. "Let me show you what I found." He stopped in front of what appeared to be a walk-in refrigeration unit. There was a square swipe card pad just to the right. Scott grabbed the badge around his neck and ran the card through. "Show time, partner."

State of the art, indeed. Scott led him to the middle of the room where several metallic devices were stationed. He opened one, which looked like a high-tech dishwasher. Then, he removed several glass slides and placed them on a small foam pad in front of a computer workstation.

Patrick stared at the equipment. "What is that?"

Scott pushed a few buttons on the ergonomic keyboard. "This beauty is called a…" he paused, appearing to want to spare his friend from useless terminology. Then, he patted Patrick on the shoulder. "This thing just analyzes blood…and matches it to a host. We have three stations like this."

Patrick leaned in. "Dr. Krieger was *quite* clear she couldn't match the blood from Azure's fingernails."

Scott rubbed his chin. "Maybe the sample deteriorated. That girl's body was out in the elements for a *long* time." He tapped at the keyboard. "Anyway, after you called, I grabbed several samples. I also compared the candles from the attorney's crime scene with the ones from the other crime scenes…and they are not the same…you were right."

"There's one for us. What about your blood samples?"

Scott smiled. "Well it *appears* there are two blood types at the scene."

Patrick eye's widened. *It had to be the killer's blood.* "Two. That's what I figured."

Scott stared at the computer monitor. "When did you have that revelation…if you don't mind me asking?"

Patrick pulled out the folded pieces of paper and handed them to him. "Mikki Chax was the *other* girl in Collin Glover's car when Azure was killed. She drew those pictures." He pointed to the man's face on the first. "She said *he* was bleeding from here."

Scott stared intently at the drawing. "*That's* the guy who murdered the man at the condo, *too*?" He handed the drawings back to Patrick.

"I believe he's our man." Patrick nodded.

Scott scrolled through the database as a list of names appeared on screen. "These are the people who possess at *least* eighty percent of the DNA matching criteria found at the scene."

Patrick strained to read the display. The list only contained *one* name he recognized, and it *didn't* belong to the *Holiday Murder's* prime suspect. *Holy Shit*. Patrick's heart started to race as he reached for his cell phone.

"Morgan, what the hell are you doing calling me on Christmas Eve?" Commander Cromartie's voice pierced his eardrums.

"Boss, just *shut up* and listen to me for one minute. I think *we* made a mistake. Collin Glover didn't murder Azure Sutaki, Graneth Kensington, or *any* of the others, but I have a pretty good idea who did…"

CHAPTER THIRTY-THREE

Donovan Petrie enjoyed *this* place. It was a shame the building had been left to rot itself into oblivion. When he was young and *still* full of eagerness, he would spend countless hours sitting in the pews, soaking in the teachings of a wise but humble man. This was *his* refuge away from destructive and abusive foster parents who were more interested in the yearly monetary compensation in the form of a tax deduction than him as a person. He had *begged* Pastor Thornley to give him shelter from that lifestyle, and let him move into the onsite housing, but Gregory Thornley preached forgiveness for a living and always told Donovan there was plan meant for *him*.

The rejection from Pastor Thornley sent him over the edge. He decided the plan *meant* for him was at the opposite end of the spectrum. If pain and suffering was to be a part of his existence, it was *only* fair he spread its wealth to as many as possible. He decided his first would be the righteous Gregory Thornley. The man had been a fond collector of crucifixes and had reminded Donovan of *their* relevance. Donovan thought by nailing *his* feet to the ground, accompanied with the binding of the hands, would be the ultimate way to mock what the man had taught him. He included the four candles because his hate for people would encompass in all direction known to man. *West, East, North, and South.*

Donovan had always followed this pattern and was doing so *again* with young Ryan Thornley. The boy was in the center of what used to be the altar. He was stripped down to his undershirt and pants, and his small feet had torn when Donovan fired the nails into his flesh. The screams had excited the killer as he watched the boy succumb to the pain. Ryan sat in the chair in almost a semi-conscious state, unaware of anything *or* anyone. Donovan *almost* felt bad for the boy to have a father so self-involved with his *own* life that he was unable to protect his family. *Everything dies...including the innocent.*

He moved into position behind the boy and removed the double-edged blade from inside his coat. Donovan shook the boy back to reality. "Hey, wake up. It's almost time."

Ryan tried to move his head. "Please...don't hurt me," he whimpered.

Donovan put a finger to his lips. "Shh...you're going to be okay." *Not so much.*

The boy shivered. "I want my daddy."

So do I. Donovan flashed the blade in front of him. "I already called him for *you*," Donovan snickered.

The color in Ryan's face was quickly fading. "Sir, let me go..."

He ran the double-edged blade along the youngster's neckline. "I can't do that..."

"Why? Please don't hurt me anymore." More tears rolled down his face.

Spare me your pre-adolescent drama. Donovan grabbed his face. "Shh...let's just wait for Daddy...okay?"

Ryan nodded, then lost consciousness.

Fucking great! He slapped Ryan again. "Dammit, Ryan, wake the fuck up." Donovan was trying to revive the youngest Thornley when he felt a vibration in his coat pocket. *Yes!* He ripped the cell from his coat.

I am here...

Donovan grasped the knife as he ran to the broken window. *Where is he?* He stared at the frozen plain. The snow was free of any tracks or footprints. *He can't be here...just screwing with my head.*

His phone vibrated again.

I can see you...but you CAN'T see me!

Donovan gritted his teeth. He bolted towards the back of the building. He forced open the thin door and stepped out. Donovan scanned from top to bottom. *Nothing here, either.* "Fuck you, Brandon! I think it's time for young Ryan to die!"

His phone vibrated again.

I like hide and seek.

Don't have time for these games. Donovan screamed at the darkness, "You *still* have a chance to save Ryan. I just want *you!*"

He received a final text.

A chance is more than you have.
* * *

Brandon knew the wooded area emptied out just a few hundred yards from *his* graveyard. Donovan Petrie would be in the church, watching for *any* signs of his presence. Brandon unzipped his coat and removed the night-vision binoculars. These weren't the typical ones found in local sporting good stores. *These* were made especially for low-light conditions. The winter sun had almost turned her light out for the day, and Brandon realized his *best* chance at saving Ryan was just a few minutes away. He had to hold himself back when Donovan had screamed out in fury about killing his son. *If he wanted me, he wouldn't just take Ryan out.*

Brandon brought the binoculars up to his face. He turned one of the circular knobs, and soon, a light green background, replaced the darkness. He trained the glasses at several of the broken out windows but was unable to pick up any movement. Brandon lowered the glasses and walked towards a row of partially hidden mausoleums, looking for one in particular. *There it is.*

When he was young, Brandon had heard stories from his grandfather about a tunnel system under the church property. It had been designed to house the church parishioners in case of an attack from an atomic bomb. Brandon had walked the church grounds his entire youth, never finding any signs of existence. On his eighteenth birthday, his father *finally* divulged the location to him. Gregory Thornley *also* made it clear that when he died, the church and her secret passage would remain a secret, until God himself decided to reveal it. He had respected his father's wishes, and even though the church had seen its last days, he *wasn't* going to be the one to tear it down.

Brandon wiped away the snow on the door. The years of rust and decay had taken its toll, and the handle almost broke off when he forced it open. An overpowering chemical odor almost overtook him. *Horrible.* Brandon quickly covered his mouth as he fumbled along the wall. He located the door to the hideaway. It appeared to be made of heavier steel than the one on the exterior of the mausoleum. Looks were deceiving, and it opened with just a few tugs. Brandon felt tightening in his chest as he took a step forward. Claustrophobia wasn't something he normally experienced, but the feeling soon passed, and he was on his way.

Brandon had promised Donovan Petrie he *would* pay for kidnapping his son. He had made a mistake in bringing Donovan into *his* world. Hopefully, it was mistake Brandon and his son would be able to walk away from...

CHAPTER THIRTY-FOUR

Patrick's Morgan patrol vehicle screeched to halt outside Brandon Thornley's lavish estate. Commander Cromartie and three marked patrol units were following close behind. One of the marked units veered off and parked behind Patrick. *Almost ready to end this.* Patrick remembered the tongue-lashing Cromartie started to give him when he explained his theory about Brandon Thornley being involved in the murder of Azure Sutaki. The harsh supervisor was *only* convinced of the man's guilt after Scott Gather showed him the blood evidence and the corresponding list that identified Thornley as a possible suspect. The Commander realized even *that* was too much of a coincidence to disregard.

Patrick glanced up at his rearview mirror. The Commander and the two remaining patrol cars drove past and turned up the following street. Patrick and the patrol officer would cover the front of the house, while Cromartie and his team intended to block off alley access to the residence. Patrick grabbed his handheld radio and turned to a secure channel. *No way to escape, Mr. Killer.*

He looped the detective shield around his neck as he motioned for his back-up officer to block the driveway, in case Thornley decided he was going to flee. Patrick was fully aware of Brandon Thornley's skill set, so he knew caution was the agenda for the day.

He pushed the radio's transmit button. "Cromartie from Morgan."

The radio squelched. "Go, Morgan."

"I have position in front of residence. Any signs of suspect's personal vehicle?"

"Negative. There looks to be a white Audi parked in front of the garage. It matches the vehicle belonging to the wife. You copy that?"

"10-4. Driveway is blocked off; I'm headed to the front door. I'll advise."

"Copy that, Morgan. Again, we have no movement out here."

Patrick pointed to the location where he wanted the patrol officer stationed. The young man took his position as Patrick forcefully knocked. "New Haven Police!"

The door flung open. A dark-haired woman in her mid forties stood there. Streaks of mascara had stained themselves against the woman's tanned features. She almost fell down when she stepped outside. "God, *you're* finally here."

She's expecting us? "Mrs. Thornley, I'm Detective Patrick Morgan with the New Haven Police Department. I need to speak with Brandon Thornley—"

"He's gone...went to find our son..." Carina Thornley said, in a shaky voice.

What the hell is going on? He reached out to cushion her fall. "Something happen to your son?" Patrick asked as she pressed herself against him.

Carina nodded. "*Someone* kidnapped Ryan...Brandon is out looking for him."

Patrick lifted her up. He stared into her face. "Do you know where he might be?"

"Who would do this at Christmas? Why *my* son?" She ignored Patrick's question.

Who would commit murder at Christmas? "Mrs. Thornley, how long ago did your husband leave?"

She wiped at her eyes. "I...don't know...maybe an hour or so."

"Has he called since?" Patrick asked.

"No, *I* called and texted, but Brandon hasn't responded. Detective, I...feel helpless."

I know that feeling. "Is he driving the Mercedes?" Patrick winced as he led her inside the house. *Damn!*

Carina Thornley appeared confused. "Why would you ask *that*? I would…think so." Carina sat down on the couch. "I don't understand."

"Did he say *anything* to you before he left?" Patrick needed to get everything he could before the woman figured out they *weren't* here because of the kidnapping.

"Maybe…I may be confused, but I think he said something like, 'this is my fault.' Meaning he's blaming himself for Ryan being taken." She laid her head on the arm of the couch as she looked up at him. "Why would he say that?"

Doesn't make sense. "Mrs. Thornley, I need your help—"

"My son was taken right outside the school…" Carina raised her head and wailed.

I'm losing her. "Mrs. Thornley, do you know where he *might* look for Ryan?"

"Right outside the school, Detective…they took him outside the damn school!"

Patrick soothed his voice. "I know. I promise you, the other officers and I'll do *everything* we can to find him. But we need to find Brandon *first*."

She turned her head and stared at the ceiling. "I wish there was something—" Carina sat up. She ran her hands through her hair. Her voice exploded. "Wait a minute! I think we have something like a GPS device installed on both cars."

Patrick shook his head. "For traveling, right?"

"No…this is different."

Patrick rubbed his face. "What do you mean?"

"It gives you the location where your car is…if it's missing."

A tracking device. No fucking way. Patrick leaned in. "Do you know what company it's with?"

Carina Thornley leapt from the couch. She ran to a bookcase on the opposite side of the room and yanked open the glass doors. "I put the packet in here…it's gotta be here!" She rifled through the shelf's contents until she found what she was looking for. Carina handed a thin blue pamphlet to Patrick. "This is them."

Patrick flipped open the front page and typed the number into his cell phone. "Carina, when someone answers…tell them, you need to find your car." Patrick looked into her eyes. "Can you do that for me?"

"Yes, if it'll help find Brandon and my son."

Patrick handed her his phone as he made his way back to the front door. The other patrol officer was still guarding the front. Patrick nodded. He reached for the radio and hit the transmit button.

"Cromartie from Morgan."

The radio clicked with static. "Morgan, we are still in the alley. No signs of activity towards the back of the residence."

"Head up front. Suspect is not on premises. I may be able to locate. Will advise when we meet."

"10-4," the gruff Cromartie responded.

Patrick reversed direction and was just about to step through the doorway when Carina Thornley almost knocked him over. She was clutching a piece of yellow notebook paper. Carina thrust it at him. "Detective, Brandon's car is at this location. The customer service person said it hasn't moved in over an hour."

Patrick gazed at the address. *Why is that familiar?* A somber look crossed his face. "This will help." He pointed to the officer still positioned at the door. "Stay with Mrs. Thornley until the Commander talks with her."

The officer nodded as he escorted Carina back inside.

Patrick reached into his coat. He withdrew his notebook and flipped though until he came across an address which appeared to be close in proximity to the one Carina Thornley had just handed him. *Why was Brandon back at the crime scene?*

Commander Cromartie had emerged from the back of the house as Patrick pulled him off to the side. He showed him the notebook, along with the yellow piece of paper. Cromartie stayed behind with Carina Thornley, while Patrick and two uniformed officers set out on a mission to finally put an end to Brandon Thornley's murderous reign…

CHAPTER THIRTY-FIVE

Darkness had come to greet the visitors of United Ministries. It wasn't the usual kind, which followed the routine pattern of sunless winter days. *This* was something else. It was more like two lost souls battling each other as even *they* realized the victor would *still* be exiled into eternal damnation. Donovan Petrie felt the frigid wind pierce his flesh as he zipped his jacket to its highest point. He huddled next to the last retaining wall that time and Mother Nature had left in tact. *Where the fuck is Brandon.* He scanned the interior, waiting for signs of the man, but between the occasional burst of snow being sent through every open crevice and the chaotic breathing of Ryan Thornley, it had turned deathly quiet.

Donovan knew the longer he waited, the more likely *all* of them would die. He was *also* well aware that Brandon had much more training and experience in these types of scenarios, but Donovan *still* had a wild card, and he was hoping Brandon's obsession with saving his son would cause him to act with impulse and recklessness. Donovan removed the blade as he crawled along the wall. He peeked out the broken stain glass, but all he saw was his Caprice as it stared at him from the other side of the street. He knew if the local police were to run a records check, he wouldn't be able to explain why he was here, and there would be no saving grace like the *first* time. *I have to end this fast.*

Donovan stood up and walked a few steps away from the window. He still had a good visual on both doors that led into the sanctuary, so it would be guaranteed suicide if Brandon *did* come from that direction. Donovan was so focused on *those* doors, and the way Brandon Thornley *should* have to travel to reach him, he failed to account for where Brandon *actually* entered the sanctuary. Donovan heard a shuffling sound coming from behind him. *Oh, shit.*

He whirled around, but the harsh glow of a muzzle flash alerted him too late. The first bullet caught him in the upper chest, sending him reeling backwards. The next two pierced his abdomen, causing blood to stream down the front of his body and onto the frosted tile.

"Ah…Ah…" Donovan screamed as he slumped to the ground. His head pummeled the floor as the bones in his face snapped with authority.

* * *

Brandon Thornley stepped out from behind the baptismal chamber, high above the sanctuary. He stared down at Donovan. *Game over.* Brandon kept the weapon aimed on the man as he descended down the stairs. The kidnapper's body jerked several times before it relaxed, and then, there was no movement at all. Brandon rushed passed him and knelt down next to where Donovan had placed Ryan on display. He set the gun down, as he reached up to check his son's pulse. The boy's skin was ice cold, but the weak heartbeat told Brandon he was *still* fighting death. Brandon quickly removed the barbwire shackles as he ripped off *his* coat and placed it around Ryan. Brandon looked into the boys eyes. Ryan blinked once and flashed him a painful grin.

This is my fault. "Rest, Ryan…just rest, son." Brandon was never one to display emotion, but this was his son. Tears poured from him as he started to pull Ryan free from the bloodstained nails. He was so focused with getting Ryan to safety, Brandon was oblivious to the sudden movement a few feet away.

Picking up his son, he turned towards the exit, but before he had completed his first step, a searing pain shot through the center of his back. Brandon fell to his knee, as Ryan was catapulted from his grasp and landed on the floor. Brandon grabbed at his back, but *that* feeling was replaced with another white hot sensation. *This* time it came from the right side of his neck. *What is happening?* His stomach started to churn, and he was nauseated as state of conscious started to fade. Brandon fell on his side. A river of blood surrounded him as the pale and broken face of Donovan Petrie came into view.

"Hurts a little, huh? Those *were* my best knives." Donovan removed something from around his torso. He limped over to where Brandon was and looked down where Brandon had shot him. *Fuck.* Blood had completely saturated the front of his clothes. He was becoming weaker at an alarming rate and *soon* would join the ranks of the dead. He dangled the bulletproof vest right in front of Brandon before he catapulted it among the debris. "Didn't count on that, did *you*?"

No, but soon it won't matter. Brandon winced. He tried to speak, but blood oozed out instead, and his words were garbled.

Donovan collapsed on the ground next to him. He stared at Brandon as *his* breathing started to fade. Brandon used all of his strength to crawl towards his son, to see his face for *one* last time, but he was too tired, and the blackness started to take him. *Too far away.* He struggled with his coat pocket but was able to wriggle out a small red envelope. He flipped it in his son's direction. Brandon exhaled one more time before the darkness engulfed him, and his journey in *this* world was complete…

CHAPTER THIRTY-SIX

This is where Brandon Thornley has to be. Patrick Morgan hit the steering wheel as he pulled his unmarked behind the snow covered Caprice. *Tell me that's not who I think it is.* He exited the car and approached the vehicle. He cleared the snow off the rear license plate. The personalized plate of Donovan Petrie stared him dead in the face. Patrick knew the man was on Brandon Thornley's payroll, but it didn't explain why *he* would be here. Patrick clicked a button on his portable radio.

"Morgan to Officer Peyton."

"Peyton here, sir," a woman's voice said.

Patrick aimed his flashlight in the direction of the church. "I have an abandoned late model Caprice across from the church. You locate the Mercedes yet?"

"Sir, it's parked on the gravel road adjacent to the property." A loud squelch interrupted the transmission. "Nobody in the vicinity, sir, but I have a set of footprints heading into the woods.

Into the woods? "Take Officer Hanigan with you, and check on it, *but* be careful. The suspect is to be considered armed and dangerous."

"10-4, sir. We'll advise."

Patrick scanned the ground. A fresh coat of snow, was blanketing the earth, so if Donovan Petrie *had* come this way, it would have been before the storm. *Only one way to find out.* He lumbered his way through mound after mound. When Patrick was about fifty feet from the church entrance, his portable radio came to life.

"Peyton to Morgan."

"Go ahead."

"Sir, we followed the prints to an old mausoleum. There appears to be some sort of tunnel here."

Footprints going in, but none going out? They led somewhere. "Gotcha. Stay at the exterior of the mausoleum. Don't wander into the tunnel. I have *no* idea where it goes. You understand?"

A few seconds passed before Officer Peyton said anything. "Roger. We will secure the area." Her voice seemed to deflate.

"10-4. I'm in front of the north entrance. I'll keep you posted, if I locate anyone."

"10-4." The radio went silent.

Patrick tightened his grip on his firearm. As he approached the door, chills swept through his body in such a way that he almost had second thoughts about stepping inside. *Christmas Eve heebie jeebies.* Patrick took a deep breath. He grabbed the iron handle and pulled at the door. It creaked open to reveal the interior foyer of the sanctuary. A set of stained glass double doors was directly in his path. He scanned to the left and recalled the staircase he had accessed when responding to the Jamie Brooks homicide. Glancing to the right, he saw several boxes were stacked in front of the remnants of the church pastor's administrative offices. The amount of rubble and trash that had fallen on top of them told Patrick the killer wasn't planning an ambush from there.

Patrick cautiously approached the sanctuary doors; he made sure to stay out of the direct path of anyone waiting to attack him as he entered. His pulse quickened with each step. Patrick positioned his shoulder against the door as he eased it open.

The interior was dark except for two small flickering lights coming from the front of the room. *Not fucking candles again.* He clicked on his tactical light and aimed it toward the dancing lights. *What the hell?* Patrick almost dropped the flashlight as he stopped dead in his tracks. *Oh my God, not all of them.*

The body of Caprice owner, Donovan Petrie, was the *first* one Patrick saw. It appeared from the small wounds in his stomach, he had been the victim of two gunshot wounds. He was outstretched on the ground, and it appeared there was something in his right hand. Patrick moved in a little closer and realized it was a heavy duty kitchen knife. Patrick gazed at it. *Just like the one at the scene of Jamie Brook's death.* Patrick walked a few more steps as he gripped the gun even tighter. The next body belonged to the *Holiday Murders* latest prime suspect. Brandon Thornley was approximately ten feet away. He was face down, a pool of blood surrounding him. There were two large knives plunged into him, with only the handle blades visible. *Bastard got what he deserved.*

Patrick closed his eyes at what he saw next. A partially clothed young boy, close to ten years in age, was just a few feet from Brandon. *This is his son.* The boy was on his side and was facing away from his father. The flesh around his wrists and feet were torn, and it appeared blood was still seeping from the wounds. *Still alive?* Patrick rushed to his side. He bent down and listened for signs of life. Patrick ripped off his jacket and wrapped up the boy's bleeding feet.

He reached for his radio. "Detective Morgan to dispatch."

"Dispatch here, sir," A young male answered.

"I need an ambulance sent to United Ministries Church. One male youth severely injured."

"Inside the abandoned church, sir?" the man asked.

"10-4. Yes, *inside* it, dispatch."

"Um...roger that, Detective. A unit will be routed to your location."

Patrick turned and looked at the two bodies. "10-4. Also, I need the Medical Examiner for two DOAs*." So, Donovan Petrie kidnapped Thornley's son...but why? The kid has the same injuries as our other victims. That doesn't make any sense. Unless...*

A short pause ensued before the dispatcher returned to the radio. "Understood, sir. Will advise when M.E. is on their way."

"10-4." Patrick reached down and tucked the coat that covered the boy tightly around him. He radioed Officer Peyton to assist with securing the scene, and soon after, she and Officer

Hanigan were there leading ambulance personnel to his location. Patrick stood up as the paramedics took over. When they removed the coat from around Ryan Thornley, a red envelope fluttered to the floor. Patrick scooped it up. He squinted to read the writing on the front.

For Ryan, my son.

He watched as the paramedics rolled the young Thornley away from the crime scene. Patrick stared at the envelope for the longest time until he realized that *whatever* was inside may hold answers that would help *him* understand. He tore open the seal to a reveal a Christmas card. There wasn't any writing on the front, the way most *usually* had. There was just a warm scene involving a father and his son. Smiles covered their faces as they stood in front of a snowman. What endeared the picture the *most* was the way *both* of them had a hold of the black top hat as they worked together to finish their winter creation. Patrick flipped open the card and read.

> *Dear Ryan,*
> *I'm sorry for everything I have done. I have hurt many people in my life, but you're the last one I ever wanted my evil hand to touch. Go to Grandpa's grave. They are there...bodies of people I hurt. Tell Mom and your brother I love them. I do love you, son, and will always.*
> *Dad*

Patrick reread the third line. *More victims of his madness?* He put the card back inside the envelope, glaring at Brandon Thornley's corpse. *You won't be able to hurt anyone ever again.*

Patrick tapped a number on his cell. "Hey, it's me...Brandon Thornley and Donovan Petrie are *both* dead."

"Donvan Petrie? The guy you were so hyped up about for the Azure Sutaki murder?" Commander Cromartie asked.

"Yes...*him*. Looks like Petrie kidnapped Thornley's kid, *but* don't know why...*we* may never know."

"How's the boy?"

Patrick sighed. "Touch and go. He has injuries similar to the ones on all of our victims. Nailed feet and barb wired wrists."

Cromartie coughed. "Thornley did that to his son?"

"No, looks like Petrie snatched the kid and did this—"

"Wait a minute...Petrie wouldn't know about those murders, or how they were carried out, *unless* he had something to do with them—holy shit!" Cromartie's voice cracked.

"Right, I think that's our answer. Commander, if you're still with Mrs. Thornley, I need *you* to ask her something." Patrick explained what he was looking for; a few minutes later, he was out the door and on his way to uncover Brandon Thornley's final secret.

CHAPTER THIRTY-SEVEN

The illumination of red and blue bounced off the snowy surroundings as the patrol units surrounded the hidden graveyard. Patrick Morgan stopped at the mausoleum Officer Peyton had found. *Maybe this is his grave.* Patrick grabbed a knife and cut away the winter foliage that was covering the nameplate. *Damn, this isn't him.* He repeated this at three more similar structures; each failed to reveal the name he was looking for. He trounced through the pine trees, looking for *anything* resembling a headstone. Patrick walked several feet before he saw the outline of a dark grave marker. He bent down and brushed off enough snow to read the name. Patrick slammed his hand against the ice.

"Where are you?" Patrick shook his head and noticed the large frame of Commander Cromartie push through the pine trees.

"Nothing, I take it?" Cromartie stared at Patrick snow covered glove. "You'll break your hand if you keep doing that."

Patrick rolled his eyes. "Thanks for the tip. No, *we* haven't found anything at all." Patrick sighed. "You would think it *should* be close."

Cromartie folded his arms. "Thornley's wife said it was away from the other graves...so it's here somewhere."

Where? Patrick frowned. "That's all she told you?"

Cromartie shoved his hands in his pockets. "That's it...oh, I heard the boy is going to pull through."

Finally good news. "I wasn't sure." Patrick moved to the next headstone. While he was clearing the snow away, his portable radio screeched. "Officer Peyton to Detective Morgan."

Patrick eyed his supervisor. "Go ahead, Peyton."

"Sir, I think I may found *something*."

"Where are you?" Patrick clicked the transmit button.

"Another set of pine trees, about three-hundred feet ahead of you."

"10-4. We should be there in a minute."

"Affirmative, sir."

Patrick and Cromartie fought their way through a maze of drifting snow banks. They spotted Officer Peyton at the edge of a small hill.

She motioned for them. "I think this is him."

Patrick rushed to her side. When he first saw the partially broken headstone, he figured it was *just* another failure. But as he drew nearer, a feeling of satisfaction came over him. The stone was very simplistic as it was only a portion of the size of most he had discovered up to this point.

Cromartie tapped him on the shoulder. "This him?"

Patrick and Officer Peyton cleared away the snow. He nodded, as he gazed at what had been written.

Gregory Brandon Thornley
April 19 1954 - Dec 21 1994
The Verse Gregory Lived By.
John 3:16

Patrick kicked at the ground. "The bodies are *here*."

Cromartie raised a brow. "What a freak…the same place as his father."

"His own sadistic way to honor the man." Patrick motioned for Cromartie to follow him, out of earshot of Officer Peyton. He pulled out the red envelope and held it out to his supervisor. "*Here's* what I told you about on the phone."

Cromartie was hesitant to receive it at first but finally grabbed the thin cardboard. He flipped it open, his hand covered his mouth as he finished reading. "How many do *you* think are down there?" Cromartie's eyes widened as he turned and gawked at the ground. It was like he was waiting for the devil himself to rip him away from the living and pull him into Brandon Thornley's lair of doom.

Patrick turned to see the County Medical Examiner walking towards them. He sighed. "We're about to find out…even if *we* don't want to…"

* * *

The hallways of New Haven Children's Center were vacant, except for the occasional nurse who traveled from call light to call light, tending to the needs of the bedridden. Detective Patrick Morgan stopped at the information desk. One staff member was packing up the Christmas decorations, while the other appeared to be engrossed in the daily paper. Patrick stood there for several seconds until the gray haired woman inadvertently glanced up.

"Oh, sorry, just reading about those horrible killings. A tragedy, indeed."

To be exact…there were twenty-two tragedies, and of course, Collin Glover was the first one found…all created by Brandon Thornley and Donovan Petrie…

She stuffed the paper under a stack of medical charts. "How may I help you, sir?"

Patrick smiled. He reached into his coat and removed a red envelope "I'm Patrick Morgan. I just wanted to give something to Ryan Thornley…if he can have visitors?"

The woman's eyes fixated on the envelope. "Are you immediate family?"

"No." He flashed the detective badge. "I'm a friend."

She eyed him with suspicion. "You're the one that found him?"

"Yes…maybe I should go…" Patrick turned away.

"No, *you're* a hero to that boy. You may see him, but promise me it's *only* going to be a few minutes?"

Patrick smiled. "I promise."

She pointed towards the hallway. "He's down the hall in room 316."

My favorite number lately. "Thanks. I won't be long."

Patrick walked down the hall until he was at the edge of Ryan's hospital room. Patrick tapped at the door before he walked in. "Hello, Ryan. I'm Patrick."

Ryan was on his side facing the opposite direction. He was staring at the small LCD screen, appearing to have all his energy focused on the cartoon figures coming from the screen.

Patrick grinned. *Everybody likes SpongeBob.* He moved closer and this time waved at the young boy. "Hi. You like that show?"

Ryan turned towards him with a sad look. "Dad and I used to watch it together."

The devoted serial killer father. Patrick nodded. "Ryan, do you remember me?"

"You found me at grandpa's church." Ryan forced a smile.

"I did. Ryan, I'm not going to ask you anything about what happened until you're ready...okay?"

"I would like that..." He turned back to the T.V. "Mom was here. All she did was cry the *whole* time."

I don't blame her. Patrick pulled a cushioned chair next to the bed. "Ryan, I found *something* your dad left at the church."

Ryan scooted up in the bed as a deep smile crossed his face. "Really?"

Patrick handed him the red envelope. "Looks like a card."

The boy ripped it open; pieces of red littered the floor. He stared at the outside for the longest time before he gently opened it. Ryan's face beamed with happiness, which given the ordeal he had experienced, was a positive sign he would resume a *somewhat* normal life. Ryan held it out to Patrick. "See what Dad wrote me?"

Son, he didn't write it. Patrick reached out for it. The card's exterior was the exact replica of what Brandon had left Ryan at the church. Patrick smiled as he gazed down at the warm scene involving a father and his son. The *same* smiles were covering their faces as they *again* stood in front of a snowman. But for him, Patrick never got tired of seeing the way *both* of them had a hold of the black top hat, working together to finish their winter creation. He flipped open the card as he read.

Dear Ryan,
You are my pride and joy. Son, I love you with all of my heart. I look at the picture on the front and see us instead. Merry Christmas...
Dad

He handed the card back to Ryan. The boy clutched it to his chest, knowing this was *all* that was left of his father. Patrick waved as he left the room and started back down the hallway. In time, Ryan Thornley would *want* to talk about what had happened, and Patrick would be there to help him sort it out.

Patrick exited the hospital. He reached to unlock the patrol car when something across the street caught his eye. A shabbily dressed older man was standing on the corner, holding a sign above his head. The sun's glare caused him to squint as he tried to read what it said. *Not again.*

Patrick walked across the street towards where the man was standing. The older man chuckled when he saw him approach. "Hello, sir. What do you think of my sign?"

"Tell you the truth...I keep seeing this *everywhere* I go lately." *True indeed.*

The man put down the sign. "Ah...sounds like *someone* is trying to tell *you* something."

Patrick shook his head. "*You* might be right."

"Oh no, not me..." The man reached into his pocket and pulled out a small white book. "You ever read it?"

Never. "My wife does."

The man winked. "But not you, eh?"

"Not so much."

The man held it out to him. "Maybe it might be time."

Who was this guy? "I don't know...I'm not a real spiritual person."

The man rubbed the stubble on his chin. "Don't have to be. You know, a wise man once told me something…"

Patrick smiled. "I thought *you* were the wise man."

He held up a hand. "Not me…I'm just an old man carrying a sign around." He laughed, which caused him to cough profusely. "Anyway…like I was saying, a wise man once told me…you can sometimes find your destiny on the road you traveled to avoid it."

Sounds like a postcard. "Insightful stuff." Patrick looked at his watch. "Hey, I have somewhere to be. Sorry to take up your time, but I was just a little curious."

The man pushed the white book towards him. "Take it then…feed your curiosity."

He had seen his wife read this book every day and maybe twice a day since Kelsey had gotten worse. Not *once* had she blamed God for what had happened. Not for the miscarriages, and definitely not for Kelsey. Why should he? *What would it hurt?* "Okay." Patrick pointed to the sign. "Would you show me where to find *that* in the book?"

The old man winked again, then reached over and turned it to the page Patrick was looking for. He folded down the corner of the page. "Here you go."

Patrick nodded. "Thanks. Maybe I'll see you again."

The man grinned. "I'm here Monday through Sunday, holding up this sign, so *I'm* pretty sure you will."

"Until next time, then." Patrick waved as he opened the car door and sat down. He stared at the book the man had just given him. He didn't know what drove him to open it, *but* he did, and for the *first* time in his life…Patrick began to read…

The End

Jeffrey Martin is currently a law enforcement officer in the Midwest. Using a strong law enforcement platform, he creates terrifying tales in the suspense/thriller and horror genres. His first two novels, *Lucifer's Calling* and *Deadly Demented*, follow a killer bent on vengeance. Two of his short stories, "Dead Holiday" and "Red, White and Blood," follow Mark Blankenship, Chief of Police and all-around trouble magnet. Another of his short stories, "House of Misery," is available as a free read on the www.jeffreymartinsnovels.com website. Jeff has begun working on his fourth novel, *Weaving Evil*.

When not working and writing, Jeff enjoys spending time with his wife and three daughters.